Summoning Spruce

Ann Ornie

www.annornie.com

Paperback ISBN: 979-8-9857515-0-5

Ebook ISBN: 979-8-9857515-1-2

For permissions contact: annornie@gmail.com

Printed in the Unites States of America on SFI Certified paper.

Editing- Kristy Phillips

Cover - Designed by Samantha at Magical Book Covers

First Edition

For my husband Shawn.
Thank you for always believing in me.

Fall

It had been quite some time since Aldo had checked this particular spot. Given the right amount of moisture, the Pacific Northwest should have been prolific with chanterelle mushrooms, but the summer had been warmer and drier than usual, leaving all his favorite spots dry. Spruce and pine needles now littered the ground after being shed weeks before by trees forced to let go of excess in order to conserve what moisture they still had.

This did not bode well for Aldo's search. His body was bent and tired from years of mill work, and now that the mill was closed, Aldo's days had simplified to a pinpoint of existence.

A few trips onto the old logging roads had come out zero. The day before, a fall rain had come fast and hard, dousing the parched soil. The droplets had hovered on top of the ground in half-moon globes. Most of the rain rolled downhill, coalescing with other droplets, running into drains and ditches. But some sat for a blissful moment and then, as if accepted by the earth, sank with a sigh beneath the surface.

It was those droplets that kept Aldo awake. If some could get into the mycelium, perhaps a few moist chanterelles would rise.

He tossed and turned all night. Finally, he rolled out of bed and put on thick socks, hiking boots, and a thin green sweater. He tied a rain slicker around his waist for luck. He grabbed his curved mushroom knife—which had a soft, bristled brush on one end—and placed it into a small wicker basket. He gently placed the basket on the bench seat of an ancient blue-and-white striped Ford F150 with rusted wheel rims and a pockmarked floorboard, and headed into town.

He first stopped at the gas station for coffee, making small talk with the clerk. But because mushroom hunters are notoriously suspicious and paranoid, he was careful not to give away where he was going as he gassed up the truck and pulled out of the station. After driving intentionally the wrong way, he circled around the downtown area and headed out to an older honey hole that his instincts told him might still have some gold left in it.

Most people had forgotten that the logging road existed. It was just over the border of the Mayback Woods, tucked below a small range that had been logged before the borders had been drawn. Chanterelles love second-generation forests, and though this forest was well past that stage, the ground called to him. Mushroom hunters learned to listen to that voice.

As Aldo crossed the border into the Mayback Woods, the land and trees seemed to change. The people on the edge of the wood lived in a cluster of buildings and gardens that wove into the edge of the tree line in a place they called The Row. They lived differently than he had as a logger and a miller in the town of Spruce. The people of The Row managed the woods as stewards of the land, opting for conservation over harvest. The trees and forests were older, they rose taller, and the land felt more alive than anywhere he had been before.

The old blue gate, which marked the logging area for recreation, was grown over, rusted through in many spots, and was no longer visible from the road. But Aldo knew it was still there. He parked his truck back between a large snag and a few young, bushy pines. If Aldo did find any, he didn't want to risk giving the location away to someone who might not respect or appreciate them as much as he did.

Increasingly in the last few years, he'd come across picking spots that had been destroyed. The mycelium just below the surface had been gouged and pulled up, disturbing the fungi below. He'd suspected youngins, at first —picking and not understanding how the mushrooms grew. But as time went on, Aldo realized that the damage wasn't being done naively but blatantly. And the only reason he could muster was that a disrespect for or resentment of nature caused the abuse.

Aldo slipped past the derelict gate. His hiking stick sunk into the underbrush that was green and thick with hearty salal and sword fern interspersed between established spruce that grew in rows.

This is what lumber does, he thought. The companies engineer nature, and he was grateful that nature had pushed back creating its own organization.

Sounds of a healthy forest filled in the space around him—the wind through the trees, small songbirds moving through the underbrush, the light static of life. Eventually, the logging road narrowed to a thin game trail dotted with berry-filled bear scat. It signified a nearby clearing that had allowed sun-loving berries to ripen.

He was getting closer to the honey hole. The forest floor was springy, cushioned by seasons of shed branches, leaves, needles, and cones. The last part of the track was much steeper as it rose to meet the range. The temperature of the woods had dropped at least five degrees.

Aldo stopped to organize his basket and tools. He leaned heavily on his stick, taking a couple pulls from a canteen. Hiking made a man realize what his body could or couldn't do anymore. It was a living mortality that he'd seen denied to too many by poor choices, accidents, or disease.

Moving around might not feel like it used to, but it sure as hell felt better than being six feet deep. He stood taller, straightened his back, and took in a wide-angle view of the woods around him. The sun rose from the east and glowed through the trees, creating haloed silhouettes of dripping moss and saplings wet from the previous night's rain. It painted the perfect picture of what nature was: a cycle. The older he got, the more he felt akin to the aged, craggy elder trees and conk-covered snags. It didn't make him sad but instead gave him a feeling of peace and hope.

His hunting spot was just over the next ridge. The last few yards were difficult because of incline and debris. As Aldo reached the top, he knew his instincts had been spot on. Golden-orange caps poked through thick moss. Its cover saved moisture below, holding conditions just right for the chanterelles.

"Wee-oo!" he whispered, and a salty rumble of a laugh followed. He used the stick to lower himself to the forest floor and rested the basket next to him. He then started to pluck, clip, and brush clean the debris from the mushrooms, finally placing them into the basket.

Fifteen minutes passed, then twenty. His basket filled at a steady pace. Aldo navigated the terrain to find the chanterelles tucked under the cover of fallen alders and pinched between ferns and huckleberry bushes, the berries long gone.

He felt the company before he saw them. Two large crows rested on the lowest branch of a spruce not twenty feet away. A third bird bounced on a branch in the tree just beyond its friends.

It struck Aldo more than odd. It made his hair stand on end. There was no reason for the crows to be here, below the canopy. Not unless there were other people nearby who had attracted the birds with their food. He sank back to rest on his haunches and took a moment to listen, realizing that not only was there no noise of people around but that the woods and crows themselves were silent.

Instinct sprang up through his body, converging below his jaw. A knot of anxiety throbbed above his breastbone. It was time to go. He rose, trying not to appear rattled to the birds. He made sure his movements were calm and controlled, trying not to give away his awareness of them. Inside, his subconscious had taken over, piloting his body toward the game trail and away from the birds, which had held his eye contact with more presence than a common crow should have.

The adrenaline peeled back years of abuse on his body and gave new life to creaky joints.

He knew the crows were still behind him as they winged between the branches. The whisper of their beating wings and the catch of their claws were the only sounds.

The truck seemed father away than he remembered, and Aldo was growing concerned. He was sure he should have been back to his rig by now, but the longer he navigated the terrain, the more he realized he must have caught the curved end of the trail too soon. Instead of going toward his truck, he was now on the east side of a larger switchback —a good thirty minutes from the gate.

He stopped. Reason and experience told him to reassess and retrace his path. The unease from the birds seemed now to be a manipulation. He took a swig of water from his canteen and tried to ease the tension that was tightening across his chest.

The people of The Row were a kind sort of people, and the woods held nothing he should fear. But he knew something was wrong. Terribly wrong. He leaned back and looked at the surrounding trees and bushes. He didn't see the birds, but the trail seemed darker and not familiar. And all the while, the silence behind him threatened to swallow him whole.

Winter

It was rare for snow to fall so close to the ocean, but Markus Wainwright had been hoping to catch photos of snow, if and when it did begin. Sea level, where the town of Spruce was, would not be his best bet. So he dressed in layers, grabbed his camera with a few different lenses, and slipped his double-layered feet into waterproof boots.

There was a lookout that faced southwest above the town, but first he had to hike a short ways to a trail covered in debris from the alder trees' fall shedding. The bare trees, now only trunks, bowed over the trail like rib bones bleached white by the sun. Through them, Markus could see the incoming storm clouds, rolling dark gray and heavy with moisture.

He kept reminding himself to watch where he was stepping. Recent rain had created mucky puddles that were now thinly frozen. The puddles could break under his boots, dropping him into a thick, muddy sludge.

Small western wrens skipped below the bare brush and salal, trying to find worms and seeds that had not yet been pillaged. But soon enough Markus was alone with his thoughts and his own rhythmic breathing. He imagined himself as a train chugging through the woods, leaving puffs of steam behind. He knew from experience that a smooth log lay alongside the trail ahead and would serve as a good place to catch his breath.

The lumber clear-cuts were the freshest here, stretching toward the eastern horizon. *What a waste*, he thought. Most of the timber that had been raked from the hillside was taken off in large, smoking trucks to mills where it was stripped, processed, and loaded into triangle piles in the mill yards.

Then the building bubble had burst and the logs never sold. They sat still in uniformed piles with grass and surf pine seedlings growing up and through the cracks in the blacktop.

It was ironic but tragic. Markus had hunted here as a boy with his father. There had been a stream that dropped out between two ridges. It had been their lucky spot to fill their hunting tags each year. But after the lumber company had sprayed a caustic cocktail of pesticide and herbicide to keep the Scotch broom and alder at bay, many elk had become lame with hoof-rot. Their offspring naturally migrated to different ranges. The spring had moved underground, with no trees to cover and cool it, and the cleft remained empty and silent.

A banana slug stretched across the path, making Markus wonder if their sticky bodies would freeze as the temperatures continued to drop or if evolution had helped them adapt and that was why they were sticky. He smiled and pulled out his camera, taking a moment to set it to macro to take a photo of the creature before moving on.

As he crouched to focus the camera, the call of a barred owl made his head snap up. It had been quite close. He'd heard them before, usually at twilight, but never before at midday. Rising, the picture forgotten, he scanned the mix of trees around him, surprised to see three large crows perched in an alder not ten feet away. Their small black eyes shone with surprising intelligence. One bobbed, its beak pointing down as it rose and fell on black twiggy legs.

Without a doubt, they were looking specifically at him. Perhaps they'd been following him, hoping for a spare snack when he sat to rest. But, as he focused on them, he could sense that something wasn't right. They watched him keenly, making no noise.

No noise.

With a start, he realized the forest around him had become eerily silent. No other birds, no wind, only a cushioned stillness that chilled him. Something was terribly wrong.

Everything in his body screamed, "Run!" and he listened. He was no longer worried about puddles or footing. Adrenaline propelled him down the short series of switchbacks to the edge of town and, finally, through his own front door.

It wasn't until he was locked safely inside his home and the chill receded from his toes that he felt silly. *Who runs from crows?* he wondered. He decided not to mention his overreaction to anyone, especially after the first flakes of snow began to fall, never knowing that as the snow fell, it covered the slushy prints of three crows that had landed soundlessly on the railing of Markus's front stoop.

It had been so very silly, until Markus heard two men gossiping at The Spruced Goose Coffee Shop two weeks later.

"No one knew she was missing ..."

"So much blood ..."

"Such a shame."

Markus leaned toward the two men in front of him in line. "Pardon me," he said. "I couldn't help but hear. Did something happen?" His voice was quiet, as he realized that he might not want to know the answer.

The men turned to him. Their eyebrows rose in surprise and their mouths hung open in a gross display.

"You haven't heard?" said the man who used to work at the butcher shop. "They found a body at the river above town!" His voice rose with excitement.

"It had no blood left in it!" the other man, with a piggish face, squealed. Their eyes were hopeful with the chance to shock him. Markus, the silly man afraid of crows.

"Who—who was it?" Markus stuttered. But all he could think was, *Not me! Not me!*

"So sad," said the one man.

"Tragic," said the other, nodding.

Markus wasn't sure which man had said the name aloud, but he did remember the slicing pain as the smiling face of Abigail Steele, a young Ironheart from town, flashed behind his eyelids. "Tragic," he agreed.

"S-sad," he stuttered as he backed toward the door and to theedge of the street, where he retched up an empty stomach that no longer wanted coffee. His vision began to shrink to a small point, and the bell above the coffee shop door kept dinging as people passed him.

Abby. A young girl not even fifteen years old.

He retched again.

Spring

THE GIRL LIKED to think that the woods themselves called to her—that the trees, plants, and waters beckoned her. Yet, as she gently moved along the forest path, wearing her favorite winter coat and hat, she still wasn't sure what had drawn her to the river so early in the morning.

Snow from the mountain range was melting into the river, making it bitter cold. Its current, swift but lazy, left large resplendent rolls that slipped over rocks unseen just beneath the surface. Later in the season, as the snow disappeared and the heat of the summer sun nipped the boughs of nearby evergreens, these rocks would stand like sentinels above the water line, a gateway to the waters beyond.

The deciduous trees around her were still barren. But when she looked closer, she noticed that the very top branches reaching toward the bright morning sun were swollen with delicate green buds. Spring had silently arrived. This made the girl smile as she admired the songbirds that fluttered between branches, trying to warm their small bodies against the sharp air.

The girl, so transfixed by the activity of life around her,

did not notice the slow, insistent creep of the chill through the soles of her shoes or the dampness of the ground beneath her knees. It wasn't until after the birds had stopped singing that she became aware of the dark cold that had crept in. So distracted by the promise of spring, she felt the danger far too late. Too late to react as a figure, larger than her own small frame, approached. Too late to regard the staccato sound of knife to bone. Far too late to stop the frantic puffs of breath as her life drained bright red into the ground below and her eyes stared vacant into the canopy of trees above, filled with birds that began to sing once again.

Chapter One

Nothing could have prepared me for the sight of Abigail Steele as she laid motionless in the last night's snowfall. Her scarf trailed to the side like ticker tape soaked in blood. It was a macabre still life of being caught in the wind, but there was no wind and no sound, save for the skittering of debris as it slid, displaced from the trail above.

"What do we know?" asked a small man in a Spruce Police Department uniform. He had soft cheeks and bushy eyebrows.

"We know she was safely in bed on Friday night, but her room was empty by ten when her brother was sent to wake her for breakfast," another officer stated.

Their features were sharp and streamlined. No wrinkles on their clothes, no lint on their gloves. They were precise. Non-Magical.

"What time was she last seen on Friday night?" Officer Bushy Eyebrows asked. His uniform was snug. The belt funneled his large upper body to spindly legs.

"Nine o'clock," someone replied.

Somehow, Abigail had left her home to be found a full mile into The Row.

I cleared my throat and spoke. "When I realized the victim was an Ironheart, I contacted you."

Officer Bushy Eyebrows nodded and scratched his forehead with a knuckle.

As a rule, Sprucers weren't Magical. Old timers on The Row liked to call them Ironhearts. Old stories told that the hearts of normal "men" contained more iron, which made them unable to tap into the natural energy of the elements. On the flip side, it meant that we could.

I swallowed clumsily and tried to ignore the sandpaper texture of my mouth as I looked at her again. My fingers rubbed the loose, knitted loops of my gardening sweater where they poked out beyond the end of my jacket. I looked like a twenty-something girl with a thrift store budget and less like the official Council liaison.

I squatted down next to the body, mindful not to touch the soil with anything but the soles of my shoes.

A feather had come to rest in Abigail's copper hair. There were no birds in the bushes or trees nearby. It felt wrong to know she had been dead long enough for events to have already happened that she would never know.

I had seen Abigail a few times here and there in Spruce. She might have come to The Row for a festival. I had a flicker of a memory of seeing her at a spring ritual, but it was only a snippet and too vague for me to be sure.

What I did know was that I couldn't help her now. I could only find the source of the dark magic that stained the ground below her and clean its energy. If I did my job correctly, only I would remember the signature of her death.

Soil touched with Blood Magic was off-putting, like clashing harmonics. Ironhearts would naturally avoid the area, but people of The Row would be drawn to it like sharks to chum. Dark imprints were intoxicating.

"Officers," I said, breaking the silence. "Please let the Council know when you're finished here. I'll need to cleanse the ground as soon as possible."

Eyebrows nodded, still rubbing his forehead.

I stepped back, making a wide arch as I scaled the ridge to the parking lot, trying to get the image of the feather out of my head.

Beatrice, her wavy hair like silver thread, was waiting for me in the idling Vanagon. "You okay, Swell?" she asked through the slightly rolled-down driver's-side window. Tangy smoke floated out of the opening, hovering in the air above the van. It was the smell of Beatrice, my hippie grandmother.

"Tip-top," I deadpanned, hopping into the passenger seat. "Starting early?" My eyes landed on the hand-rolled joint smoldering in an abalone shell on the dash.

"One can never cleanse the space too early," Beatrice replied, her eyes bright but her brow furrowed. "It's my own blend. Mullein for pain, passionflower for insight, and sage for clarity. Perhaps I should have added lemon balm..." Her voice trailed off as the van lurched forward. She guided it out of the lot and onto the highway, toward Spruce.

The coastal highway cut through a state park and climbed the northern side of Mayback Mountain. It opened wide to skirt a sheer basalt cliff that rose above the road for over a hundred feet then dropped off to the sea two hundred feet below. It was a breathtaking sight, even for those who of us who had lived here our whole lives.

As the Vanagon puttered along, the air through the open window moved the checkered curtains in waves, and the dreamcatcher that hung from the rearview mirror swung back and forth like a pendulum. Beatrice was talking out her plans for the day and the clay she was planning on throwing later, but I wasn't really listening. My mind kept floating back to the feather, so black it was blue in contrast to the girl's pale lips.

The dark magic that had taken place next to the river was strong—stronger than I had experienced before—and it lingered like a whisper just below my skin. The death of a Non-Magical would affect The Row's relationship with the citizens of Spruce, and if Ironhearts were now being killed by magic, there would be a problem. I pulled at my sweater's thread, curling and twisting the loose loops absently as I looked out toward the ocean.

Just on the other side of the cliff face, the road quickly descended past The Row toward town. The cluster of homes that grew into the tree line above Spruce were a natural mix of limbs and roofs, leaves and eaves. They moved in a flow of color and texture and magic. The small houses were made of cedar, hemlock, and spruce, and each was set apart with an artistic flair. Some had red shutters and ornate rock fences, while others were modest with gardens overflowing in abundance. Laundry fluttered on clotheslines in the distance as we passed. It was such a normal, everyday thing, but the day was anything but routine.

Beatrice easily navigated the stiff steering of the van as she spoke with animation, her hands and arms moving, taking turns holding the steering wheel as she spoke. Though well over sixty, her eyes were youthful and full of a life force that seemed to glow out of her. Each wrist was sheathed in multiple bangles of assorted metals that tinkled softly against each other as she spoke. She was a wisp of a woman. No more than five feet tall and twelve inches wide.

If she stood sideways, you would lose her behind a lamp-post. But what she lacked in size, she held in presence and delivery. She didn't hesitate. Her instincts were impeccable, and she ruled with an iron spoon. If you wanted to be fed, you made damn sure you stayed in her good graces.

My brother, Finnigan, and I—both in our mid-twenties—still lived with her. It was quite common for generations to live in one house on The Row. In exchange for room and board, we helped with chores and handy fixes around the property. We mended fences, maintained the duck pen to keep the predators out, cut wood, weeded the beds in the spring, and then harvested for canning in the fall.

In truth, Beatrice didn't need the help. It was we who needed the normalcy and ritual of her home. She was our glue after the death of our mother.

"Beatrice?" I said, interrupting.

"Yes, dear?" she replied, eyebrows pinched in question.

My heart felt heavy from what I had seen at the river. I didn't want this to bring danger to The Row. To our family. To Beatrice. "I ... I love you."

The bracelets on her wrist jangled as reached out to touch my arm. "I love you too. Everything all right?"

"Yeah ..." I wanted to tell her that I was worried. That the dark magic still lingered in my hair and on my tongue, as the metallic taste of iron. "I'm going to have to borrow the car," I deflected.

Beatrice chuckled. "You scared me, Swell. Of course you can have the car. I'll just have Finnigan pick me up after yoga."

"Thank you," I said, smiling to ease her mind. "Try not to break any hearts, okay?"

She laughed away my teasing with a swipe of an arm. "Those men need some excitement in their lives." She pulled the van up to the curb across from The Spruced Goose and turned the ignition off. "Remember, I need the van by eight to make it to the Goods for moon meditation at nine."

"I remember," I said as I took the keys from the ignition and we both got out. I watched her walk across the street and through the park to the yoga studio. I didn't feel better even after I saw her go inside the yoga studio and the door shut behind her.

Chapter Two

Spruce was a logging town that had lost its boom. It had only taken a slight dip in the economy to kill the lumber industry. Near the water, mills sat empty—their offices silent time capsules of ugly brown chairs, orange walls, and metal desks waiting for people who would never come back.

Just east of town, clear-cuts stretched like a plague through the coast range. The land had been poorly managed, and now nature was taking it back, rising up through rotting stumps overrun by Scotch broom, alder, and blackberry. There was a comforting justice to it all.

Despite Spruce being a poor town, residents still took pride in their homes. The storefronts were welcoming, lampposts were adorned with appropriate holiday decor, elementary schools still sang with the voices of children at recess. There was one gas station, a small supermarket, a coffee shop that doubled as a laundromat, and one bar. It was a town that refused to die.

At the intersection, an old brown Chevy truck passed in front of me, broke my line of sight and brought me out of my head. The driver waved, lifting his fingers up in salute from the wheel. I nodded and smiled. Would Sprucers be so friendly when they learned about Abigail? I looked both ways and then stepped out into the crosswalk.

The building that housed the local post office and The Row Council office had the appeal of an abandoned bank. The exterior was smooth brick that was sun bleached to a faded brown.

The reflection in the tinted glass of the front doors distorted shape. I could see that the dark-brown hair I'd braided in haste this morning was loose. A halo of flyaway hair circled my heart-shaped face. Tapered black denim pants were tucked into well-worn boots. A thick wool jacket crisscrossed my chest and was clasped together by three copper clips. They looked nice but also served the purpose of small energy boosters for some of my more difficult spells. It was hard for some people to take a grown cherub seriously, but I couldn't help my face and I wouldn't sacrifice comfort.

The main level of the building was your standard-issue post office, but the sub-basement housed The Row's Council office and it was their attempt at integrating with Spruce. They had tried to make it look "normal," but even the waiting room had a flair for the artistic, with a river rock mosaic floor and richly stained wood tables and chairs. The reception desk was a large section of tree trunk on its side, that had been smoothed by wind and salvaged from the river. Where the traditional flower or potted plant would have been, a square glass terrarium glimmered softly. Inside, spruce needles hovered. They shimmered as they gently dismantled into their elemental components and then spun to reassemble into tender green needles once again.

Just past the desk, a short corridor of offices spread the length of the building. The second-to last-office on the left was mine: the home of Reconnoiter and Determinations, which was a fancy way to say research and "un-spelling" for when things went just a little awry. Most people called my department R&D to my face, but behind my back they called me "the cleaner." To the Row Council, I was just a maid who tidied up behind them.

A neon-pink While You Were Out memo was tacked to the message board outside my office door. It looked harmless, but it never was.

I unlocked the door and dropped my backpack onto the couch inside the office. The memo, filled out with feminine handwriting, directed me to see Elder Todd as soon as was possible.

Instead of going directly there like a good dog, I busied myself with turning on the computer and inspected the inch of coal-black water I'd forgotten to empty from the coffee carafe the day before. I pondered chancing it as a headache pushed from behind my eyes.

I opened the window to let in the sounds of the wind as it moved the limbs of the pine trees across the street. I sighed in resignation and popped a handful of candy from the dish on the desk. into my mouth and started another pot of coffee.

Elder Todd had been on the Council for as long as I could remember. He never seemed to be getting anything done, but he was always happy to take credit for everything that was finished.

I didn't like him.

I already had enough to do, filling out reports and writing up my findings regarding Abigail. Just the thinking of her made the sweet in my mouth turn sour.

"Ah, Swell!" Elder Todd said as he entered my office without knocking. A frizzy mane of gray hair and a long beard were the focal points of the Chief Row Councilman. "Did you happen to get that memo?"

I leaned back into my chair and kicked my boot up on the desk. There was a small intake of breath from the half rate Santa.

"Gosh, I sure did, sir. But I've just been inundated with that DBA case in the Mayback and emails."

He shifted and leaned against the wall, his eyes gauging my honesty. I ate another handful of candy.

He smiled. "Yes," he said. "Thanks so much for your help with that." His eyes narrowed. "I know it's late in the day, but we've received another tip regarding possible blood magic being used. We're going to need you to follow up on it."

I sat forward, "Okay..."

"It came in as a possible poaching case, but the Council was consulted in light of recent events." He waved away the last part of the sentence with a flick of his pale fingers.

My hackles rose.

"In light of recent events," I repeated slowly. "You mean the death of an Ironheart?" I shook my head. What a shitty way to minimize the murder of a child.

He cleared his threat. "Yes ... that. So we'll need you to make sure that the poaching is just a poaching."

"I see. And if it isn't ... just a poaching?" I knew my words said business, but my tone implied that he was an asshole.

"Take care of it." Turning to leave he said, "I'll have Diedre, give you the details, and you can head out."

A witty retort stuck in my throat.

Take care of it? Two acts of blood magic done within twenty-four hours wasn't something to just "take care of." Blood magic was not only illegal, it changed the caster forever. In return for that sort of magic, something had to lose its life. It wasn't something that could be undone.

Right now, in this town, Abigail's family and friends were mourning her. For the person took her life, she had just been an ingredient. Something to be "taken care of." The bureaucracy of Elder Todd's statement floated down like a feather and stuck to my mouth.

THE PARKING LOT WAS MOSTLY EMPTY, SAVE FOR A FEW police vehicles that remained. The location information of the poaching tip was rather vague, but had guided me back to the same area where Abigail Steele had been found. The caller had stated that they had found the deer off trail and east of the river.

After the logging bust, The Row elders had addressed the county board with folders full of environmental impact reports and EPA violations in the Mayback Woods. As a part of the agreement, the folders were sealed. But there must have been substantial claims because the county deeded seventy-eight thousand acres of prime timber to the people of The Row in perpetuity, which was not a small feat.

From the parking lot, I could still see the crime scene tape. It moved soundlessly in the breeze, which made the hair on the back of my neck rise. A cloying, coppery scent of darkness moved in the space that was marked as a crime scene. It pulled at me stronger than I wanted to admit. I popped another handful of candy into my mouth and turned away.

I needed to be sure-footed, silent, and quick. I wasn't really sure what I was walking into, and because of that, I'd called Finnigan to see if he wanted to come along. He hadn't answered his cell and he hadn't called me back, which was odd.

I pulled a small daypack filled with necessary herbs and fresh water from the back of the van and grabbed my hiking stick. I shut the Vanagon door softly and when no one was near, I gently stepped off into the brush and let the forest close in around me. There was no better camouflage...

The woods were filled with the nervous energy of the coming spring. Squirrels, chipmunks, and birds hungry from a long winter chattered and scrambled as they scavenged nuts and seeds revealed from the melted frost. Birch and alder trees, tipped with light, spread upward. Green shoots of new growth peeked through on their tallest branches. In a clearing, well off the trail and out of eyesight, I crouched down to the ground and gently swiped the leaves and duff from the top of the soil.

I took a moment to look around, then pulled out a strand of my hair and pushed it into the soil. Grounding to the forest's mycelium would give me compass-accurate direction. I slipped off my shoes and socks and stood directly onto the coolness of the exposed dirt. I wiggled my toes and imagined branches and roots sliding down from me into the loam. Quicker than electricity, they reached out to the neighboring flora. My strongest root anchoring well into the bedrock and core of the mountain with a comforting tug.

I took a deep breath, pulling the familiar dampness of the woods down into my chest, focused my intent, and spoke within my head. *I'm here to locate wrongdoing within the wood. The death of black-tailed deer. Any help would be appreciated.* My will reached out to the cells beneath the surface, hopping and skipping along the connections within the soil. It moved much farther than I could on foot—and far more effectively.

There was a slight delay. The woods stood still. I'd reached out, but I wasn't guaranteed they would have an answer or choose to help. These connections were complicated, and I had to respect that.

I didn't have to wait long. The answer was subtle but obvious as the ends of my hair rose, pointing directly northeast. "Thank you," I said with a nod, as I picked up the smooth hiking stick and moved in the direction my suspended hair now pointed.

Chapter Three

The going was much slower than expected. Following the direction my hair pointed was a good idea in theory. But in reality it meant I had to slog through waist-high salal that grew ruthlessly up the hillside at a forty-degree angle, all with my hair in my face.

Nice work, Swell, I thought.

I needed to be more mindful next time. Earth magic was especially literal. If you asked for directions, you were going to get the answer that the earth understood.

At the crest of the ridge, a game trail skirted a barren clear-cut. The land seemed to curl into itself, the trees bending inward to heal the wound. I paused for a moment and noticed the different stages of regrowth, as this was the only area where the Mayback touched land still owned by an active logging company. There were no sounds. No birds. No wind. There was only the ragged sound of my breath in my ears and the smooth reassurance of the worn hiking stick in my hand. I moved on, weaving down the backside of the ridge.

I reached the top of a craggy ravine and caught sight of

the deer across the wide expanse on the opposite side. It laid on its side, the legs rigid and body firm with bloat.

In order to reach it, I would have to go down into the ravine forty feet and then find a way back up on the other side. Daylight was beginning to fade, the twilight dangerously softening the surroundings. If I didn't know what I was stepping on, I could fall or get impaled very easily. It was the nightmare broken ankles were made of.

Thinking I could reach the poached deer off trail before the sun went down was a rookie mistake. As the dark came, I couldn't help but remember that I was less than a mile as the crow flies to where a young girl had lost her life just hours before.

The Row Council required reports of blood magic to be followed up on as quickly as possible, but I shouldn't have been so naive. The park was rugged. It had taken me twice as long to get there slogging through the bushes. Light would be gone soon, leaving me at a crucial disadvantage. Not to mention, I'd miss family dinner and I couldn't have that.

My only choice was to scout the route first, then scale down the embankment and hope for the best. I grabbed another handful of M&Ms from my pocket and popped them into my mouth. I looped the hiking stick to the back of the pack so my hands could be free. My stomach growled. Chocolate always helped, but Beatrice would worry if I didn't make it home for dinner. I needed to get a move on.

The descent was slow but steady. As I reached the bottom, a rumbling from the tree line above caused me to crouch down beside the trunk of a young spruce. Someone was coming.

In an explosion of noise and motion, a large dog the size of a small horse broke through the brush above. Its eyes were wide in panic as footfalls of people careened after it. "Get back here, you dumb bitch!" a voice shouted after the mutt.

The fawn colored dog barreled toward the open space of the ravine and tumbled down the embankment, leaving tracks in the clay as she slid, falling hard into a stump with a sickening thud. There was a yelp as the wind was knocked out of her.

"That fucking mutt can't do anything right. What kind of hunting dog don't hunt?" said one of two men as they stepped clear of the tree line. The leader stopped short, causing his shorter and hardier cohort to slam into him from the back.

From the look of it, both were freshly done with logging shifts, still dressed in camo jackets, high-water jeans (more brown than navy) that were held up by thick suspenders, and scuffed steel-toed boots. But they came with a different kind of tool: each held a thick-stocked rifle, over their shoulder.

I could intervene and place myself directly in their path to shield the dog, or I could wait it out. My gaze slid to the limp dog, who by the looks of it hadn't had a true meal in weeks.

I'd never been a "wait it out" sort of person and with a reluctant sigh, I stood.

"Evening boys," I said from the base of the ravine, loosening the hiking stick from my pack.

Clearly the men weren't expecting anyone to witness their pursuit. Startled, the taller man swung his gun toward the sound of my call. "The fuck you doing out here, girly?" The man said as he looked past me to search the ravine for anyone else. "You all alone?"

Two smooth river stones weighed lightly in my pocket.

Both held energy imprints set by the latest full moon. They would be a shame to waste on the two, but it was comforting to know they were nearby. I had brought friends after all.

"You seen a dog?" the short one asked from behind the taller man.

"A dog? I thought you were looking for a bitch." I smiled.

The taller one, realizing I was alone but not afraid, scrunched his face in irritation. "Got a mouth on you, don't cha?" he said lifting his gun to menace. "Ain't a man never taught you to keep your fucking mouth shut?" His tongue ducked out, wetting his bottom lip, and exposed his yellowed upper teeth.

I shrugged, sliding the stick down to touch the ground. "What fun would that be?"

The force of one's intention is usually too broad. If you were able to channel it through an object, it could be far more efficient. That's why so many people claimed to think of someone just before they called. And that intention can go either way. In this case, using the stick to impress my intention allowed me to directly focus my will to them.

The dog stirred slightly fifteen feet below, dislodging debris that tumbled down like bones. "You hear that, Frank?" the smaller man said. He shuffled forward looking over the edge. "Stupid mutt's gone and hurt itself. Ain't no good to ya now."

"Larry," Frank said, "go on down there and fetch that dawg."

Without hesitation, Larry set down his gun and nimbly scaled down the tangle toward it.

"Stop," I whispered, moving the command into the ground, speeding it to the decaying trees Larry was scrambling across.

"Sit," I said quietly.

Larry froze mid-step then slammed his rear down to the tree trunk, displacing bark dust into the snag below.

"Good boy," I whispered.

"Gawd-dammit, Larry! Stop messing around and get that mutt!" Frank wasn't used to being disobeyed.

"It looks like Larry's had a change of heart," I called out.

Frank's face pinched in rage. He leveled the gun at the dog, who was now awake and cowering in fear. "She's no good to me anyhow." His finger looped in to press the trigger.

I leaned into the hiking stick and focused my command through it. "Fetch."

Larry leapt up, running full tilt toward his friend, who was now retreating.

"Larry! No! Get back!" Startled and off-center, Frank tumbled back, landing hard on his backside, with his friend on top wrestling for the gun.

Using this as my chance to get to higher ground, I climbed the clay and snags toward the top. The dog followed behind me, her movements stiff. From the opposite side, I could see the men in a tangle of camo and dirt.

A shot rang out, reporting across the forest startling all of us. All of us, except for the dog, who was on-point waggling her butt at a very pissed forest ranger standing at the tree line's edge.

"Drop your weapons!" he shouted. "You are all under arrest for suspicion of poaching. Get down on the ground!"

Chapter Four

There was a dive burger joint in the older part of Spruce. It looked like time hadn't moved past 1972. The cement walls were painted red, white, and blue, and cartoon ice-cream men decorated the menu boards. Everything was greasy, cheesy, and gloriously deep fried. In no way was anything there good for you, and I couldn't stop thinking about it.

I was almost to the point of hallucinations and well past hangry when the forest ranger, Bronson Wise, unlocked the makeshift conference room door at the park's ranger station. "You are being released with no charges," he said.

"I told you a hundred times, I was R&D for The Row Council. A hundred! You could have listened to me."

He leaned against the doorframe and smiled. "You think you're the first to pull the 'magic' card while in the woods, Miss Swell?"

I rolled my eyes. "Did you really have to handcuff me? I was unarmed."

"Unarmed? I wasn't born yesterday. I know what a hiking staff can do." Bronson shifted his weight.

"Do all Ironhearts insist on doing everything the hard way, or is that just you?" I grumbled as I slipped past him into the hallway.

"You can pick up your personal belongings at the desk, but your dog and van are in impound."

"My dog? I don't have a dog!" I said, turning.

"Well, you do now!" he called over his shoulder. "Congratulations..."

IMPOUND WAS ABOUT A MILE DOWN THE HILL FROM the ranger station. As I walked, I called Finn to let him and Beatrice know that I was okay. But to also let him know that, no thanks to him, I'd been arrested by a rabid park ranger and was at risk of starving to death. He didn't seem surprised.

"Yeah, the ranger called to verify your address and employment with the Council," he said.

Of course he did. "So you're answering his calls?" I asked. There was silence on the other end of the line. I cleared my throat. "Did Beatrice happen to save me dinner?"

"She did, even though you left her stranded without a car."

Shit. I'd forgotten about the moon ceremony.

"Seems she was expecting an army," Finn continued.

"Was it burgers? Please say it was burgers!" My stomach ached.

"With cheese."

I squealed with delight. "I'll be home in thirty and I'm bringing a friend."

When I reached the impound office, it was closed and

an emergency number was taped to the window. I called the number, but it went to a fax line.

"Are you kidding me?" I said, kicking at rocks with my hiking boots. I was hungry, smelly, and pissed. I just wanted the Vanagon and a burger. Was that so much to ask?

I rang the number again. Maybe if I became an annoying pest, the dispatcher would actually pick up the damn phone. After the fourth attempt, success.

The voice was familiar. "Miss Swell?"

Ranger Danger Bronson Wise's voice grated my patience. I felt the space around me charge with my energy. It pushed out past my skin, crackling with the atoms in the air.

"Get. Me. My. Van. Now." I spoke each word with bite.

"And your dog."

I weighed my irritation and hunger.

"Fine."

"Wonderful. I'll be right down." His voice was smug.

The farmhouse was dark by the time I got home. The dog hadn't strayed farther than a foot or two from me since she'd been released. She was horrendously underweight and galloped along in an uncoordinated gait. A dull fawn coat hung loose over her bony frame. I thought of the two men who'd had her just hours before, and I didn't want to think of what could have happened to her if I hadn't been there. What sort of person didn't feed an animal? I shook my head. Not a good one.

"Solis," I whispered, pulling just a smidgen of solar energy through the house's roof and beams. It made the ceiling glow lightly, like it was catching morning light.

You'd think a group of magical hippies would have installed solar power by now, but The Row's elders felt that it would be too demanding of nature. Harnessing and storing the Sun's power for later use was too close to slavery of the elements.

I'd argued that solar panels weren't much different than moonstones that held energy for a specific purpose. Solar panels would simply absorb energy not being used on the structures. Why waste it?

Elder Good had grumbled his disapproval. "Nothing offered is wasted," he'd said. My suggestion had been dismissed with no further discussion.

Using the glow from the roof, I used my fingers to help guide me to the kitchen. The smell of ground coffee steered me through the hallway. It was a full moon, after all, and the kitchen glowed coolly from the light filtering through the canopy of old-growth trees that thrived within The Row. I fumbled in my pocket for the stones and placed them onto the window ledge where they could soak up the moon's energy.

"Beatrice!" I called out. "Where are the matches?"

"Matches?" I heard her reply in surprise. "Why in God's name don't you use magic?"

Because I was tired, but I didn't want to say it out loud. It'd been a shit day, and I wanted to leave it at work and not bring it into the house.

I leaned my stomach against the kitchen counter to steady myself in the dim. Slowly my eyes began to acclimate to the light. The contents of the kitchen began to take form and edge around me. I could see the ancient propane stove (which didn't seem safe around a community of people continually learning their craft through trial and error) and the counter-to-ceiling shelves crowded with glass containers and books with paper bookmarks sticking out at all angles. There were dried-flower bunches crisscrossing the ceiling above me like prayer flags. Even decanters of soil and branches sat upon the countertop. The room smelled of the earth.

I crouched low next to the stove, focusing on the tea kettle. I poured in roughly two cups of filtered spring water, then gingerly turned the propane valve counterclockwise. The smell of gas was instant.

Taking a deep breath, I focused the intention of flame from my mind out to the very tip of my right pointer finger. I tapped the air once, connecting with the invisible gas. "Incindus," I whispered, hearing the will of my intent connect with a pop. The flame glowed bright, bringing shape to the gas.

The spell took the last of my energy.

"Did you find the matches, Swell?" Beatrice asked. She carried an oil lamp, casting a warm yellow light around her. I suspected she had purposely taken her time bringing the light.

Beatrice believed that Ironheart technology was a crutch I used when lazy. She was right. "No. I used my finger," I said.

She nodded, setting the lamp down on the counter of worn butcher block. "Good. I have a plate fixed up for you and for your new friend." She lifted the lantern to illuminate the dog at my side. "She's quite thin, poor girl."

I retrieved a plate of food from the fridge and pulled apart a juicy burger still warm at the center. Finn shuffled in from his room upstairs. His hair reminded me of a guinea pig. It stood on end from one central cowlick on the back left corner of his head. He'd been asleep while I walked in the cold. What a brat.

I tossed a piece of the hamburger near the dog's front feet. She sniffed it but didn't eat. Large eyes and a wet nose rose to search the air for a more interesting scent. She padded over to the counter, nose almost touching a potato wedge on my plate. "You want that?" I asked. There was a faint tail wag. "Well, go ahead," I encouraged. Her head tilted and she delicately pulled the potato down onto the floor. It was gone before I could blink. I took a plate from the cupboard, scooped the remaining wedges onto it, and set it onto the floor, where it was devoured in record time.

"Well, she knows what she likes. Reminds me of someone else I know," Beatrice said, giggling and turned retreating back to her room.

Finn leaned his hip against the kitchen counter, one hand hooked in his pocket and the other ran through his hair. "What did you find?" he asked.

"You mean before or after I was arrested?" I snapped. My voice was harsher than I'd intended. I was hungry and tired, but that wasn't an excuse. "Sorry." I rubbed my eyes with my knuckles. "I'm not mad at you. I just wish I could have inspected the deer before that jerk ranger arrested me like a criminal."

"Don't worry about it." Finn's hands raked through his hair. "Even though you didn't inspect it, you didn't sense any blood magic, did you?" His tone was concerned.

I thought back to the ravine. To the dog and her paws scraping through the clay. The smell of the trees as the shorter man had stepped on it. I could taste the soil in my mouth from impressing my will through it, and I knew there hadn't been any magic there, blood or legal, before mine in a long time. The deer had been poached. I told Finnigan my impression.

"Well, that's great news," he said. "It's possible that

Abigail's death is a singular incident. Maybe from a spell that went wrong."

I thought about that. The longer I was away from the scene, the more I knew deep in my gut that Abigail's death had been intentional. It had been murder and I was worried.

Chapter Five

I STOOD on the front porch, wrapped in my favorite sweater, and watched the dog sniff and search for the perfect spot. The sound of wind through the trees drew my attention to the top of a thick-trunked spruce tree. Its branches were heavy, gnarled, and covered in moss, and as the wind blew in, it rattled the dried needles and cones. They fell as the spruce danced, swaying like the ends of my mother's skirt.

I hadn't thought about my mother in quite a while.

I only had a few memories of her, but what I did have always came with the price of memories I wished I could forget.

My mother had been beautiful, smart, and funny. When she had failed to return from a forage, we hadn't been alarmed at first. Beatrice had attributed it to the coming full moon. There had been a list of things my mother had wanted to harvest and perhaps she'd stayed with a friend in town. Phones on The Row were rare at the time, and there wouldn't have been a way for our mother to let Beatrice know she'd been delayed.

When she failed to return the next morning, we all knew something was wrong.

As children, there was nothing we could have done and so we were packed into puffy coats and heavy knapsacks and sent to school. Beatrice had told us our mother wouldn't want us to worry and that she wouldn't want us to miss school. Afraid but brave, we held each other's hands and walked to the edge of The Row to catch the rattling bus that would take us to school in Spruce.

Since Finn was older than me, he'd been unable to walk me to my classroom. The feeling of my small hand leaving his felt more meaningful than before. I felt alone for the first time.

I stood watching him leave as the bustling of bodies down the long industrial hallway swallowed him up. My hands were sweaty, my coat too warm, and my bag too heavy. A feeling of overwhelming loss roared within me.

I startled as another hand had joined mine.

"I'll walk with you." The voice belonged to a short blond girl. She smiled and nodded encouragingly, putting on a brave face. "You can sit with me today. I've got cheesy crackers I can share."

I moved with her, carried along in a disconnected haze to the kindergarten classroom that now felt too bright and too colorful. I spent the day hoping my feelings were wrong, knowing with a bone-wracking certainty that my world would never be the same.

I'd known that our mother wasn't coming home. I'd known it from the moment a small black feather had floated past the window of my room the night before.

As the school day progressed, it became easier to ignore the truth, to avoid it. The normalcy of the daily routines had distracted my mind. Looking back, I wish I could have stayed naive just a little longer. To be safe in the unknown. But all of that optimism was shattered by a third grader swollen with ego at the knowledge he possessed.

I NOTICED SOMETHING WAS DIFFERENT IN THE cafeteria when the dull roar of children eating and talking began to be replaced with the eerie hiss of whispering and then silence.

I was focused on my lunch of chicken nuggets when a voice I recognized broke out from the other side of the room.

"That's not true!" Finn's voice cut through me like glass. "You're a liar!"

I stood and spun to see where he was as a clatter of lunch trays and bodies moving drew my eye.

Finn had lifted another boy simply by pointing at him. The children who had been seated next to them just moments before pushed back and away from the threat.

"It's true!" The large boy in blue jeans three sizes two big and a Raiders football jacket shouted, refusing to back down. "Your witchy mom is dead!"

"My mother isn't dead!" Finn screamed as his eyes turned a glossy black.

The realization that something horrible was happening coiled in my belly, and I scrambled over the table bench seat and down the aisle, skidding as I turned the corner and cut straight for my brother. His right hand continued to point at the boy while the nails of his left hand dug into his palm. A red smear that didn't look like ketchup stained his pant leg. His right hand's fingers were splayed out like rays of the sun that I'd drawn in class before lunch.

"Finnigan," I said, pulling on his black coat. He didn't

seem to notice I was there. "Finn." I pleaded this time, both of my hands pulling at his arm that raised the boy without touching him. All of my weight hung from him, but he didn't budge.

Teachers were flooding into the cafeteria now, alerted by the lack of sound. The cafeteria rang with a deafening quiet. "Finnigan, stop!" I cried. Tears pushed behind my eyes. I could taste grief but didn't know or want to understand it, to ask what it meant.

Another voice cut between us, breaking the spell my fear had cast. "Finnigan Swell, stop it this instant!"

"What is the meaning of this?" another voice shouted. I was pushed and pulled away in another direction and watched as my brother was lifted by multiple teachers. The spell, finally displaced, sent the older boy falling to the table below. Various forks and spoons, cups, and bits of food flew in the air as he landed.

My eyes searched wildly for Finnigan, whose voice cut through the clatter. "My mother is not dead!" he screamed, and as they carried him through the doors toward the office, a cry erupted from his throat. It was a heart-wrenching mewl. A tortured sound. It was the sound that fawns made when they called for their mothers who would never return.

Just like our mother.

"I've got you," a small voice said next to me as it guided me to the library to cry in private. It was where I stayed until Beatrice came for me.

Finnigan changed that day. He became quiet and introverted. He didn't laugh for years after our mother's death, though I'm sure I hadn't either.

It was my first introduction to blood magic.

The rumors that floated around bordered on sensationalized propaganda against the people of The Row. Her death had occurred smack in the middle of the lumber boom and crash, and some worried her death had been a ritual to curse the people of Spruce. The people of The Row could taste the darkness of the spell, and the paranoia that someone among them must have killed her strained our already weakened bonds.

Families moved, Ironhearts migrated, mills closed, and finally the forests began to regrow without the threat of disruption.

I'd always suspected that the forests had been a present from our mother. That because she couldn't be here, she'd made sure our world was safer and our forests were ready and waiting for our adventures in life to begin.

That was, of course, just a child's mind making sense out of chaos. I'd been trying to find some sort of reason out of the horrific murder of our mother and of the magic that had fattened itself from her death. It was also my attempt at forgiving our mother for leaving, even though her departure wasn't by choice.

"Are you coming in, dear?" Beatrice's voice surprised me. It was followed by the scent of incense and the warm, earthy smell of clay.

I nodded, pulling the sweater tighter, keeping an eye on the dog, who was now casually inspecting the perimeter of the front yard.

"It's so cold tonight," I said, my eyes still scanning out past the trees to the town below. I knew the ocean lay just past it, though we couldn't see it from The Row. Magic didn't come from the sea. It ran to it.

"Do you ever think about my mother?" I asked.

She was quiet for a moment. Taking a deep breath, she pondered, taking in the view. "I think of her every minute of every day, of every month, in every year." Beatrice's hands, which were clasped together in front of her, now began to worry against each other. "She would have been so proud of you and Finnigan. Of how you both grew up." There was a sadness in her voice, but there was also a softness of love.

"Do you think her killer is still here?" I'd never asked the question aloud before. I didn't want to know the answer... and maybe because there hadn't been any other deaths, I believed he or she was gone. That we were safe.

"I'm not sure," she answered truthfully. "I do know that if they are, they will get what's coming to them. There's no doubt about that." Her long arm reached to pat my shoulder, and then I was alone.

I thought about Abby's family. How they would now spend the rest of their lives processing her death. Avoiding her death or diving into it. I sighed, the sadness a heavy weight.

The dog now sat with her eyes toward the tree line.

"Ok, doggy," I said, "time to come in."

She turned her head to glance at me, unmotivated.

This wasn't going to work. I couldn't leave her out in the cold. She barely had any meat on her bones. This time I used force behind my word. "Come."

She was unfazed.

"Here girl!" I repeated, my voice upbeat this time. "Want more treats?"

This word seemed to interest her. "Potatoes?" I asked. Her tail thunked a yes. "Okay! Come get your taters." She blew past me toward the kitchen, tongue and tail wagging.

Despite myself, I smiled.

Chapter Six

I PUT on neon-green running shoes and a thin Spruced Goose hoodie, as the dog that only answered to "Tater" barreled down the stairs in front of me toward the kitchen, where Beatrice was mixing up a batch of pancakes. Tater was no longer interested in going for a run but had zeroed in on the smells that Beatrice was creating.

"Good morning, sweetheart!" Beatrice said, tucking a stray hair back behind her ear. She wore a long skirt that moved across her bare feet.

"Morning," I replied. "I think I'm going to go for a run."

"All right, dearest," she replied, smiling. "Would you like me to save you some pancakes?" We both knew it was a rhetorical question. Even if I said no, she'd fix me a plate for when I returned.

"Yes, please." I secured my brown hair into a hasty tie and edged toward the door. I slipped the iPod into the band of my yoga pants and called for Tater. She dropped her butt straight to the kitchen floor and locked her eyes on Beatrice.

"Suit yourself," I said and slipped out the back door.

Mornings on The Row were soft and quiet. When the

fog slid between the treetops and rested within the canopy, the forest became an enchanting world that called to me. I shook off the sleep that still lingered in my body and headed toward the trail that wove inside the forest just steps from Beatrice's home.

Before I put my earbuds in, I took a deep breath, held it for the count of four and then blew it out through my nose listening to the sounds of The Row around me. Everything smelled fresh and healthy. I repeated this until I felt centered and then turned up Depeche Mode as loud as it could go, softly jogging between the garden beds, past the duck pen, and out to the ridge that overlooked the old spring that had run dry. A ghastly clear-cut spread from the other side of the ravine to the ridge across, over and out of sight. Occasionally, we could still see elk herds moving through the expanse of alder and Scotch broom, but since the rut last September, they hadn't made an appearance.

Once I got into the woods, I was able to open my awareness and run on a blissful autopilot. My body knew these woods with a sense memory that let me quiet my mind and relax. It was also when I was able to come up with my best ideas.

This entire grove had been logged before. Some saplings pushed up under the dark canopy, but the majority of the trees were second-stage spruce that rose roughly thirty feet up. Their diameters varied but averaged eighteen inches across, thick enough to make a person feel they were in a proper forest. Continuing through the trail system, I passed large stumps, the remnants of giant behemoths at least eight to ten feet across. Back in the day, loggers used large crosscut saws to slowly cut away at the trunk six feet above the ground. The planks they stood on left behind telltale notches in the stump bases. It was sad but comforting. Now that The Row held ownership of the Mayback Woods, we could ensure that these younger trees would have the ability to grow to the size their ancestors had once been.

Storms this past winter had snapped weaker trees, leaving tangles of limbs and stumps across some of the trails. It was the natural order of nature. Usually I could navigate them, climbing under or over, but because of the way the streams in the watershed wore steep crevices into the landscape, sometimes my run was obstructed with the need to backtrack and find another way around.

I couldn't stop thinking about the two poachers in the park. They had been dressed for logging. There had even been fresh sawdust in the folds of their pants and shirts, but there hadn't been logging here in fifteen years. I wanted to know why they had been so close to the Mayback Woods and why they even thought they could get away with poaching so close to The Row. Either they weren't from around here or they were just plain old dumb. My money was on dumb.

I pushed my body up the switchbacks that scaled to the top of the mountain. My legs burned and my lungs squeezed with a fire for more oxygen as I finally reached the top. The view made the pain worth it. A patchwork of tracts dotted to the north, south, and east of me, each in different stages of regrowth. The fog still moved just inside or above the tree line, obscuring a large portion of the trees in a dainty blanket of white, but I didn't feel the chill anymore.

I flopped down on the basalt outcropping and laid flat, my eyes looking skyward as the clouds, caught in an updraft, rose with speed up the ridgeline and were tugged by the jetstream. They flew past me, making me feel as if I was flying and the clouds were moving below me.

When I became chilled, I sat up and swung myself to

face west. As the sky continued to move, I saw bits of the town below me between the cloud breaks. Occasionally, I could see a crystal-clear view of the woods stretching as far as the eye could see into the coast range.

The rising sun occasionally caught a reflection off the buildings below in Spruce, but once I thought I had seen a flash from the northeast. It had been quick. When I turned to face that direction, I never saw it again. I stood to keep my muscles warm. But before continuing on, I'd need a drink.

When The Row took ownership of this land, the elders found a freshwater spring that had been in horrible shape. The clear-cutting had loosened the soil around it. When the fall and winter rains came, the sediment from the treeless slopes above had moved with the rainwater, down to choke out the spring.

Beatrice had brought us there to see the elders work to save it. They had dug with bare hands, scooping away debris, until I'd seen the crystal bubbling of water jump with life past dirt-stained fingers.

Finn and I had been nine and seven years old when we'd planted saplings in the cut above the spring and helped stack rocks and logs to reinforce the stability of the area. We worked to ensure that, until the ground became stable again, the area around the spring would remain unobstructed. Today, if I waited long enough, I could drink the very same fog that swirled around me.

There was no clear path from the rock to the spring from where I was, but I could see a faint game trail that swung outward around the rock.

The salmonberry and blackberry shoots inside the underbrush pulled at my pants. Once I passed through the wall of thick green, I stepped into a small amphitheater that hosted a now healthy spring. The water pushed up from the ground clean and cold, rolling and bubbling into a clear pool surrounded by the rocks and logs we had used to reinforce it.

Moments like this made me grateful for Beatrice's insistence that we participated in things children weren't usually allowed to do. We were able to witness the sheer force of will for a stream of water to push through the ground, to be solid but separate, with one goal; to flow to the ocean.

I scooped my hands into the clear pool and rose the liquid to my face, breathing in the essence of what made the wild possible. It smelled of greenery and stones. I splashed the water to my face, relishing in the cold shock it gave. Then cupped one smaller portion of the water and drank enough to quench my thirst.

I didn't want to leave, but I didn't belong here. No one belongs at the source of a clear spring. Its ability to be clean depended on having the least human interaction possible, but I yearned to draw as much peace from the location as I could.

A stone at the edge of the pool pulled my attention. I bent to pick it up and held it tight in my palm. It warmed from the heat of my body and physical reaction as I impressed a memory into it. Stones from places of importance and fond memory could be used for specific spells in the future. I wanted to remember the optimism and hope I felt right now.

Once the spell was complete, I placed the rock into the pocket of my pants that was the perfect size for bits of plants, pine cones, and forestry bric-a-brac.

Chapter Seven

I'd come to the garden to think. I knelt next to last year's bed and moved my hands inches into the garden soil. As I weeded, I tossed and turned the soil, over and over. The basic repetition of preparation helped to clear my mind and allowed me to think.

It had been seven days since Abigail's body had been found. Seven days of apathetic interest from superiors, and I knew deep in my gut that if I was going to find her killer, I would have to do it myself. I couldn't let Abigail's family feel the ache of the unknown like mine had.

I felt the air in the garden change and was surprised to find that it wasn't Finnigan who had joined me but Ranger Danger himself, Bronson Wise. He was taller than I remembered, but his sour expression remained.

"If you're going to stare, you can at least make yourself useful," I said, shaking free the soil from an errant buttercup.

Bronson cleared his throat, but I stayed in one spot, not wanting to give him the satisfaction of stopping what I was doing. "I have a bit of a situation," he finally said.

My head snapped up. Bronson's pale-blue eyes looked back at me. He wasn't kidding.

Well, I'll be damned.

"What's up?" I asked, wiping away a stray hair from across my eyes with the back of my hand.

Bronson's weight shifted, and his eyes were no longer directed toward me but focused on the grass near my feet. "There's something wrong on my land." The statement hung in the air.

"Wrong as in what, exactly?" I was curious but not enough to hide the irritation I felt. Bronson Wise wasn't magical. I didn't answer to him.

"The trees are changing."

"Changing?"

I could see him search for the words. "I can't see it when I look directly at the trees. But from the corner of my eye I can see something's not right. Like a dream that doesn't make sense."

This was definitely my department. He absentmindedly twisted his right forearm inside the grip of his left hand. I watched the tendons move under the smooth surface of his skin. He had my full attention now.

"Show me," I said.

THE DRIVE FROM THE ROW WAS PAINFULLY SILENT. While Bronson drove, I pulled at the cuff of my gardening sweater. I didn't know what could be so off that an Ironheart would be able to see it. Nothing with that much juice could be good. Energy like that could throw the balance off at not only Bronson's land, but many others. The butterfly effect of nature. Cause, effect, cover ass... etc., ect.

The old truck's chassis rattled along the ruts in the gravel road to Bronson's parcel at the base of the mountain. Willow, sword fern, young juicy birch, and blackberry bushes leaned out into the roadway, competing for the sunlight. Occasionally, the warm, fruity scent of sun-touched leaves passed through open windows of the truck's cabin. A couple berry vines were already in bloom. Spring was coming quickly and with it, the warmth of the sun.

The nearer we got to Bronson's land, there was a unease that flittered, too, through the windows. Whatever it was, it was affecting Bronson as well. "Can you feel that?" I asked.

"I feel edgy," he said.

"Stop."

"I'm serious," he answered.

"Stop! Stop the truck!" I yelled.

Startled, Bronson jammed on the brakes and the truck slid and pitched to a stop. "What the fuck, Swell?" He looked at me, his hands gripping the wheel.

But I couldn't break my eyes away from the view of the trees rising unnaturally above the alder and spruce.

"Those don't belong here," I said. My fingers, no longer worrying fabric, pointed north toward three ancient coastal redwood trees spearing the sky.

I had heard stories of Elementals being summoned, but only in the old tales told to scare children who were particularly naughty. Redwood Elementals were the most terrifying, unbending, and inhospitable. They could only be summoned by blood. And whoever had summoned them hadn't just summoned one, but three.

"Shit. This isn't good," I whispered.

Goosebumps rose on my arms. I fought the urge to lift the sweater's hood over my head and slouch into the seat, but they already knew we were here. No reason to hide.

"Keep going?" Bronson asked. His eyes were hopeful, but I felt sickening dread.

"No. From here we go on foot," I replied, checking my pockets for my handmade blade in its leather sheath.

Stepping off the roadway seemed appropriate. It gave the false sense of cover from the unnerving "Eyes of Sauron" observing us from above. We hadn't been granted permission to enter the wood... yet. The land was no longer Bronson's; it now belonged to the ancient trees that rose far above us.

Thick underbrush slowed our approach. I wasn't sure how close we should get, but undoubtedly the forest would let us know. Bronson was somber. His focus was toward the trees and brush in front of us.

I was surprised at how quietly he moved. His footfalls were a vacuum of sound. There was definitely a feeling of predatory stealth about him. I made a mental note to remember his scent, a fingerprint of identity, just in case.

"I'm not really sure what we are walking into," I admitted, fighting the urge to whisper.

"I can handle it," he replied.

"I don't know if I can handle it." My confession was met with silence, but his pace didn't slow. He pressed through the sea of green and stepped out of the brush first.

The air was thicker within the clearing. Needles and pine cones from the surrounding trees hung suspended in the air, inches to a couple of feet above the ground.

Moving through them created a ripple of movement in the atmosphere. It pulled at our clothes like we had stepped into oncoming surf.

Time was fixed within the circle. The trees, themselves immortal, shimmered, leaving impressions of something too beautiful to be understood and too horrible to be seen.

I didn't want to be here. I should have talked to Beatrice first. She would know what to do. But it was too late for that. The trees were waiting to be addressed formally, and if I did it wrong, we would both be dead.

I had brought Bronson with me for one dark purpose. In order to reveal the summoning's worker, I would need an offering of blood with a connection to the land. Unfortunately for Bronson, "offering" was a vague word in magical terms. The element of surprise in acquiring it was known to sweeten the deal and might earn us some favor.

Stiffly, I crossed the space between us. Bronson's head was tilted up as he observed the rough bark and branches above us. As he turned, the knife in my hand moved easily along the crest of his forearm. Pearls of blood rose immediately and glistened along the edge of the blade.

Before he could react, I slammed the knife through the suspended leaves and needles, into the soil. The beads of Bronson's blood slid to the ground, puddled, and disappeared.

It took a moment for me to register the buzzing in my ears before the concussion of the spell hit me. I was propelled backward, pinned to the ozone like boundary at the circle's edge. The trees bent toward us, but Bronson hadn't moved. The spell moved around him, parting like a sea of energy and intent, brushed aside with the movement of his tan hand.

What the fuck?

The pain as I was pressed against the boundary ward was unlike anything I'd experienced before. It was like being cooked from the inside out. Whoever had placed the spell was not only clever but vindictive.

"Jo? Swell!" I heard Bronson calling... *But why was he talking through a metal can?*

"Swell, can you hear me?" There was a painful crackling of static and the smell of almonds. "Can you stand?"

Strong arms lifted me, and I was up among the trees. Smooth-skinned branches lifted me to the sky as I coughed through the blood running down the back of my throat.

I HEARD THE TINKLING OF BEATRICE'S BRACELETS.

"Get her into the tub!" Her voice was the color of storm clouds.

I buried my head into the smell of sandalwood and tried not to melt through the arms that carried me.

People were talking, but I was burning inside. I couldn't stop thinking about Bronson's hand waving away the spell. The image melded with the smell of him.

"The water will disperse the spell, but she will fight it. The water must be cold," Beatrice said.

This didn't sound fun.

"Clothes and all?" I heard Bronson ask. I curled my fingers into the fabric of his long-sleeved shirt.

I liked warm better.

Beatrice insisted. "This magic leaves a stain. Her clothes stink of it."

I hope I hadn't ruined my sweater.

A wet muzzle pushed at my neck. There was a sneeze and then a shrill keening. *Was I crying? No. That was Tater...*

A baritone voice brushed against my ear. "I'm sorry about this, Swell." I leaned into the comfort. "Payback's a..."

Huh?

And then the warm arms released me into the ice bath from hell.

Chapter Eight

I CROUCHED GINGERLY onto an obnoxious green cushion in front of one of Beatrice's prized red onion garden beds. I wasn't just stiff, I was sore everywhere. The residual effect of the ward had fried my nerve endings and left me to fail at anything that implied movement. My skin felt like it had been left on a hot skillet.

Now that I was finally down next to the bed, I would be able to weed and recharge from the elements in the soil. I sunk my hands straight in, midway to my elbows. I sighed.

I watched Beatrice's garden ducks waddle around the end of the garden beds. Their rounded bills opened and closed as they padded and pecked their way down the path, ambivalent to me. They worked through the soil Finnigan had turned the day before.

"Hello, boys," I said as I brushed the mud from my hands and attempted to slide my fingers, that were as agile as a cold block of ham, into gardening gloves. "Good to see you again. You know, since I almost died."

The brown duck tilted his head, directing a small, glassy doll button eye at me. His feathers looked soft and I fought the urge to squeeze him like a pillow. "You ever been electrocuted?" The duck quacked, seeming to size me up.

The duck quacked again. This time he pinched the end of my gardening sweater, that smelled of bleach and iron, and pulled.

"Hey! No pulling! That's my favorite sweater," I said and smoothed the disturbed knit that now showed a hint of rust between the pearls. My blood.

"Go eat some snails and earn your keep."

The duck padded just out of reach, quacked, and shook his tail feathers.

Once the ducks realized I wasn't hiding any snacks, they moved along to forage in and around the beds. They were a good alternative to pesticides, as they gobbled up anything that ate our vegetables without damaging our crops. They were also adorable. Beatrice had named them, but as a matter of principle, I refused to use their names. Names meant you'd get attached.

Beatrice was in the house, and Finnigan had taken Tater with him to the fields while he rototilled the soil. According to Beatrice, the dog hadn't stopped howling since she'd caught my scent, covered in blood, from Bronson's truck. But between me and the fence post, I was thankful I hadn't taken her with us. She could have gotten really hurt.

I was finally alone for the first time since I'd blammo-ed myself by tripping the blood magic ward. It wasn't a rookie mistake, but I should have known better with elemental magic being used. Whoever had summoned the redwoods wasn't a novice, and I should have respected that.

Now settled next to the bed, I pinched and pulled the unwanted weeds between the onion stalks. As the sun warmed my back, I steadily piled them up to later add them to the compost pile. I loved that such a basic task was meditative enough to clear my head of how humiliating the last few days had been.

Beatrice had told me how scared Bronson had looked and how I'd been less than thankful when he'd placed me in the water. With the amount of blood I'd lost from my mouth, nose, ears, and eyes, I was surprised I'd had enough energy to fight him. After two days of sleeping, I still wasn't back to normal.

The high-pitched rumble of a Volkswagen truck let me know that Finnigan was already on his way back. So much for being alone. Before the truck had completely stopped, I could hear Tater's paws attempting to grip the gravel drive that looped to the side gate.

"Tater! Wait!" Finnigan called after her. It always shocked me how much he looked like our mother; tall and slim with tanned skin grazed with freckles along the ridge of his nose, cheek bones, and arms.

A storm of paws and tail and knees approached faster than gravity could stop, and she careened into the side of the raised garden bed. "Tater! I'm fine! I'm fine!" I said, but to be sure, she needed to lick my face and ears. "Stop. Stop, girl," I giggled. "You're going to knock me over, and then I won't be fine. Tater, calm down." Tater's rump thumped down to the ground and her tongue hung out.

"Why did you name her that? Why not something majestic?" Finnigan asked.

"Because I couldn't get her to eat anything but french fries and hash browns when I got her out of impound." Tater drooled in confirmation. "Great. Now she's hungry." I groaned as I rose.

"I can feed her, Swell," Finn said, but I waved him off.

"I need to move around. I'm only in my twenties," I replied. "No need to get a wheelchair yet." But the truth was, I was trying to sound braver than I was. My guts still felt like soup, and guts shouldn't feel like soup.

"Later, ducks!" I called over my shoulder.

"They're actually drakes," Finn corrected.

"Huh?"

"They're males. They're called drakes," he said, scratching Tater behind her ears and pointing with his other hand to the curled feather on the duck's hind end. "It's called a sex feather."

"Yuck," I said horrified. "Instead of worrying about me, my brother corrects my vocabulary." I smiled and began my shuffle to the back door to bake Tater a potato—and sneak in some salmon oil and chicken while I was at it. She followed close behind, long nails clicking on the wood floor as we entered the kitchen.

"You sound like a velociraptor with those claws," I said as she rubbed past my leg and curled into a ball on a bed Beatrice had made for her at the base of the kitchen island. "We'll need to trim those."

"I thought you didn't have a dog?" Bronson's voice startled me, and I dropped the potato. It rolled across the floor, stopping at his feet in the doorway. His face beamed a smart-assed grin.

"What kind of a guard dog are you?" I said to Tater as I tried to push away the memory of my wet clothes sticking to my skin when Bronson had placed me into the bathtub. He'd smelled of sandalwood, and now it was a memory that I couldn't shake.

Tater seemed to answer my question with silence as she licked her leg and pretended to not see me or Bronson.

"Swell!" Beatrice's disembodied voice carried from the pottery studio. "I think Bronson's here. I can see his truck!"

"A little late..." I said under my breath.

"You seem to be feeling better," Bronson said as he crossed through the doorway to sit at the kitchen island, too close to me. I could practically feel the heat of his body. I rubbed the back of my neck and moved away from him, breathing from my mouth.

"I don't remember inviting you in." My voice was crosser than I intended.

"Beatrice did," he replied. "When I saved your life, she said I was welcome anytime." He was smiling wider, if that was even possible.

I grunted. "I'll have to speak to her about that."

"I'm not here to fight, Swell," he said. He set the potato on the counter like a peace offering. "I just wanted to call on you and see how you were doing. You lost a lot of blood." He added.

"I'm as good as I can be," I said. "But I want to know why the hell the ward didn't touch you."

He shrugged. "Just lucky I guess," he replied.

"Wards don't have lucky charms," I said, cutting an X across the potato with a knife and setting it in the microwave for eight minutes. "Wards are like bombs. They affect everyone in the vicinity when they're tripped or go off. And yet you look like you just got done with a spa retreat."

His eyebrows shot up. "You think I look pretty?"

"Pretty stupid," I grumbled.

"I didn't know you had ducks!" Bronson said. His voice showed excitement as he rose to pick up the brown duck who had found the back door still open. He tucked it under his arm like a football.

"They're drakes," I deadpanned.

"You don't say."

The pottery studio Dutch door swung inward, and a fog

of incense and smoke rolled out. "It's not pot!" Beatrice called out. "I have a prescription."

"It's pot, isn't it?" Bronson mouthed at me.

I nodded.

He smiled. "I'm just a park ranger, so unless she's got a covert grow operation inside the park boundaries, I've got nothing to say on the matter." He set the drake down. "He have a name?"

"It's a drake."

"I meant the dog," he said.

"Sure SHE does." I put an emphasis on the 'she' part. "You may call her Tater."

"Tater?" he said in surprise. "Why not something ...more"

"Because she has a refined palate and I've got a small vocabulary."

I was beginning to shake. I hadn't moved around this much since I'd woken up, and I was starting to realize I might have done too much. I gripped the counter and took a deep breath, trying to make the black spots in my eyes dissipate. The baked potato was still cooking in the microwave, so I opened a large mason jar and pulled out a few kale crisps. They tasted like ass sprinkled with ranch seasoning. I didn't have enough sugar in my body, and it felt like I was vibrating.

"You okay?" Bronson asked behind me. Tater was whining, her head against my left leg.

I didn't have enough time to answer. A red-hot bolt of energy speared through me from my root to my crown. I heard my own startled cry as I tipped like deadwood to the floor. There was a swelling of pain as the black dots in my vision burned through, and a rising sensation shot me through my forehead. I was no longer seeing the kitchen but processing a blinding white light of crystal-clear pain.

THERE WAS A HOT STONE ON MY HEAD. I RAISED MY hand and tenderly touched my forehead, smoothing my hair. No rock. Just my own head thumping like a punk band.

"What the fuck?" I hissed in frustration. "Why does this keep happening to me?"

Beatrice's artist hands that were tanned and muscular, patted and rubbed my left arm. "You are just fine, JoJo," she said, calling me by my childhood nickname. Her long, flyaway gray hair circled her head like a halo. It seemed like she was glowing.

"Do I have a tumor? Am I dying?" The anxiety in me was threatening to take over.

"No." Beatrice laughed as she moved around the room. Her feet made comforting shuffles against the plank flooring.

"How did I get to my room?" I asked, realizing I was now above the studio and in my own bed.

"Your man friend carried you up. He seemed very concerned." She moved between the end table and the dresser, snapping and pruning herbs into a mortar. "I sent him to help Finnigan with the garden."

"He's doing chores here now?" He irritated me even when I was dying. "Is he living here now? Will he have my room?" I tried to sit up but settled for propping myself against the headboard.

Beatrice was crushing something that smelled like passionflower and chocolate. "He sure gets your goat, JoJo."

She laughed again. This time she turned to hand me a cup. "Hot cocoa with allies. You need the sugar, and passion-flower will help you get your energy back."

I took the cup grudgingly. There were always more herbs than Beatrice let on because they usually tasted bitter. It was better to be naive in those situations.

It felt like I'd been shish kebabbed with lightning.

Beatrice sat down on the edge of the bed. She smelled of sage and clay. "I heard stories of Elementals growing up, but I've never seen one myself." Her fingers traced a flower stitched into her apron.

"I know a place you can see some," I said stupidly.

"Magic that strong drains you."

"I know... I'm just so embarrassed," I replied.

Beatrice rubbed my arm and I handed her the now empty cup. It had gone down smooth, but now the coppery aftertaste had kicked in.

"What exactly was in that?" I asked.

Beatrice smiled sweetly. "I'll never tell."

Chapter Nine

The soreness in my body was gone, but a nervous vibration replaced it. I scanned old newspaper articles that connection to the area between Spruce and The Row, on Beatrice's ancient dial-up Compaq computer. The internet was slow enough to be knitted by thread itself.

After taking the entire time to brew a pot of coffee, a short story loaded from the Spruce News. A local mushroom hunter from Spruce had gone missing months before, and the only sign of him that had turned up was his truck. It had been parked just off the roadway, near an access road to a retired lumber tract. Search-and-rescue from Spruce had combed the area, but no other signs of the man had ever been found.

Beatrice sneakily insisted that Bronson drive me to The Row's Council office, since I was in no condition to drive. I was irritated with how manipulative she could be. But for fun, I had Tater come along inside the truck to sit between us. The cyclone of dog hair that swirled inside the cab was reward enough.

"Wouldn't she be more comfortable in the back?" Bronson asked.

"Wouldn't you be?" I flashed a grin.

He grunted.

The sun had burned through the fog that squatted low over the coastal town. Its heat warmed the exposed skin of my arms and face, and I couldn't help but sigh. The dampness of winter seemed to linger longer each spring, and I longed for the sunshine.

Bronson's truck rumbled by the houses of The Row, down the steep hillside, past the general store and gas station. At the bottom, his truck slowed to swing into the downtown area of Spruce. People mingled on the sidewalks. Some stood with their heads tilted toward the sun like dazed refugees of winter. Tater bit at the open window, her large jaws making a snapping noise.

Bronson laughed out loud. "She's a real snapping tater."

I rolled my eyes but grinned despite myself. "So you didn't grow up here," I said, more as a statement than a question.

"No," he replied. "But my family was one of the first settlers in the three-rivers region. We go way back as farmers and loggers."

"You're from a logging family?" I asked, surprised. "Your property has tons of old-growth trees on it."

He nodded.

"I wouldn't expect that from a lumber family."

Bronson leaned across the seat to open the glove box. His hand rummaged for sunglasses he couldn't see through the massive dog trying her best to impede his mission. I ended up tapping them toward his hand. "Logging isn't hereditary," he said.

I snorted. "Tell that to the trees. Clear-cuts last for generations. How is that any different than an inheritance?"

There was an awkward silence broken by the tapping of Bronson's truck keys as they rocked against the steering column.

My work for the Row Council mainly focused on Dark Magic containment and magical signatures. Occasionally, my work required my unique skills for tracking. I was able to search for an energetic signature in a specific area, in a spell, or a specific person that emitted a specific vibrational signature.

As callous as it sounded, humans did horrible things to each other every day but to have two very different incidents involving Ironhearts within the magical perimeter of the Mayback Woods, my instincts told me it couldn't have been coincidence. Someone either was using the woods to amplify their work or was drawn to it because it was familiar to them. If they were one of us, it would come to me to find their signature and then find them. We couldn't have someone slaughtering Ironhearts.

Bronson stopped the truck in front of the Council office. "Need help in?" he asked, all politeness.

"I'm good. Thanks for the ride." I gathered my messenger bag and wool shrug. Tater's hair was stuck to it, standing out khaki against the black of the coat. The dog jumped down from the cab and sat on point. Her tail swept against the sidewalk in an arch, displacing small pieces of gravel, as she watched me. I closed the heavy truck door, trying not to make eye contact with the driver Beatrice had called my "man friend."

"Call me if you need a ride home," he said as he put the truck back into gear.

"Finn can get us," I said. My cheeks burned. Was I blushing? What the hell?

His right hand saluted me as he pulled out onto Main Street.

"Jesus Christ, Tater. I'm losing my mind," I said after he was out of sight. The dog's head tipped to the left and right as I spoke. "I'm not a fainter. I swear." She didn't look convinced. "I'm a regular badass."

She barked.

"Let's get some work done, ya mutt." I scratched her behind the ears, earning a grateful thump from her tail on the sidewalk.

Chapter Ten

Usually the Council's main-floor offices had people moving about in them, but as a rule, Saturdays were very quiet. I took the time to enjoy it.

My tiny office was cluttered with books piled up on top of each other and plants in reclaimed pots Beatrice couldn't sell, on shelves. There were stones of different sizes and textures on every surface. A large glass jar filled with layers of soil from each significant place I had been to sat prominently on my desk, and pine cones of different types were displayed on counters, between jars, and on shelves that held more knickknacks than books.

A large comfortable couch took up a portion of the room. I'd learned from experience that there were only so many times I could see seventy-year-olds dance naked under a full moon before I just said, "You know what? I'll stay in my office tonight."

Tater took a running leap onto the couch, and the force of her size made it thump into the wall. "Easy, Tater," I said. She spun twice, folded herself into a circle, and tucked her nose below her paws.

I sat gingerly onto my beat-up desk chair, whose springs groaned each time I moved, and opened the interdepartmental mail folder. It was the Spruce PD case file for the missing mushroom hunter.

Aldo Fuller:
-Caucasian Adult Male
-Age 72
-Retired Lumberman
-Address: 487 Waddel Road #3 (The trailer park just below the cut zone, I mentally noted.)
-Left home for a mushroom hunt on Oct. 10
-Missing Person's Report filed on Oct. 11 by neighbor

It all seemed rather normal as far as missing persons cases went, and I could see why I hadn't been consulted. But the murder of Abigail Steele by Blood Magics inside the Mayback, a stone's throw from the same location another Ironheart had gone missing, my intuition told me there could be a connection. It was my turn to see what I could find.

"This is where the rubber meets the road, Tater," I said as I moved around the room grabbing a glass container of rich, dark coffee grounds. "Not everyone is able to track like you can as a dog. Your noses are made to sense and translate information to your brains to give you insight to your surroundings." I set the glass jar down on the counter, then poured water from a small sink, into a large electric kettle and set it to boil.

"A dog's sense of smell is forty times greater than a human's, which makes Magical trackers quite rare. The magic used is so obscure most don't understand it. Trackers like me can tap into the vibrations of the earth and recognize a person not by their looks, smell, sound, or behavior but by the actual essence of what makes them organic." I poured three heaping scoops of dark coffee into a cone receptacle, placed it over a stoneware mug, and then directly poured the boiling water over it counterclockwise to banish any barriers to my work

"I've never really explained what I do to anyone before," I said. Despite this revelation, Tater hadn't even noticed I was talking. Her large frame of elbows, joints, and nose were still neatly tucked into herself like a fitted sheet. Only the smell of the coffee, that filtered black as tar into the cup, roused her interest. I'd found the more caffeine I had in my body during my search, the better the results. But wasn't that the case with everything?

I made myself comfortable on the couch next to the annoyingly adorable hairy beast who had invaded my life and rested my feet up on the coffee table. I took a few quick swigs of the coffee and a handful of M&Ms. The sugar and caffeine hummed within me, and I relaxed back onto the couch, threaded my hand through Tater's fur, and began my descent down the rabbit hole.

At first nothing happened. My mind was too busy with questions and emotions. The events of the day and the dull ache behind my eyes kept pulling me from my task. In order for this to work, I'd need my mind to be passive and open to any images that might slide through. Anything that didn't belong was important. Ideas and thoughts that could be traced to my life and the recent days were tainted and not valid.

I could only describe the images as similar to photos that were developing in a darkroom. They floated in and out through a viscous, clear menstruum of continuity. Sometimes there were smells or sounds, but that was rare. Eventually an image took shape, like the exposed images in an X-ray. Trees, bushes, sword fern, broken bits of dried pine branches. White triangle. A rusty sign and a sound that I couldn't quite catch.

I was jerked out of the meditation. Tater stood across me, her large paws skewering my thigh, teeth bared at the wall I shared with another Council member. She began to bark at the northeast corner.

"Tater, Tater. It's okay. Stop," I said. My neighbor Henrick Miner used sound to modify technology. I'd never really thought about the high pitches Tater was able to hear that I couldn't. No one was usually here on Saturdays, so I hadn't thought... "Wanna go for a walk?" I asked.

Tater's attention didn't hold long when the bribe of sniffing things outside was dangled in front of her. She jumped down.

I jotted down my notes from the meditation on Aldo Fuller. I made an annotation to talk to Henrick about letting me know when he planned to do certain pitches of work, and slipped the paper into my satchel.

I grabbed Tater's halter, but when she saw the contraption, she immediately began to fight. "If you want to go outside, you have to wear this in town," I told her. Her front end lowered and her rump rose as she primed to jump back, directly into my herbal cabinet. "Tater Rebecca Swell, if you move one inch toward my herbs, I will transmute you into a toad!" It might have been the tone that did the trick, but she didn't move. She didn't know what I said, and she didn't know that transmuting was something only done in books, but she bought it. I tried not to notice that I'd also given her a middle name.

Once the harness was on, she didn't pull. If I hadn't

known better, I would have said Tater had been well-trained. She sniffed hands and legs as they passed on the sidewalk but all in all, she was totally polite.

The downtown area was well-kept and had businesses of different types. I'd always been proud of this little town. Each storefront was maintained and interesting; fasciae, doors, and windows were painted in bright and inviting colors. It was magical in its own way, and I found comfort in its ability to thrive despite the downturn in the logging industry.

The sun was still out, and the heat spread across the back of my shoulders, warming me from the outside in. The city park was small but had large oak trees that cast a delightful shade through their new leaves. Tater and I found a spot on the grass that was soft and not damp. I spread out, and she began to groom her paws. Laying down and looking up, my mind was able to disconnect from my surroundings and spread up through the canopy to cast a wider mental net. I swept the town and thc trailer park where Aldo had lived, and found resistance there, which made sense. His energy rose up like debris in a river. I swept the roads surrounding town in my mind, in a grid-like formation, and sensed nothing. I focused on the roads leading to The Row. His signature—which felt of hard work, piles of old newspapers, and evergreen needles—faintly pulled from the tree line. It wasn't strong enough to be recent, but it was probably the area where he had gone to mushroom hunt. I made a mental note to confirm the location.

I swept wider, across The Row toward Bronson's property, tentatively seeking. It felt like I was touching a bruise. Too fresh for me. Just as I was about to pull myself back down through the limbs and succulent green leaves, there was a tug at my mind. Strong. Then gone.

What the hell?

That had never happened before. The energy was gone. Was it possible for someone to mask their location? I'd never heard of it before, in research or in person. I swung my awareness around once more like a Doppler radar I'd seen on the television news shows. But there was nothing from Aldo. Only the feeling of dry, crisp newspapers on my fingertips and the impression that I was two steps behind the information I needed.

I heard Tater's tail thump and followed by a low rumble in her chest. A shadow blocked out the pleasant warmth of the sun on my face, and I opened my eyes.

"Sleeping in the park is against the law, Josephine Swell. You can't dirty up our park with your dirty, hippie dog."

I groaned. The voice belonged to Annabeth Montgomery.

"You sure make a wide shadow, Annabeth," I said. "How can one person block out the sun?"

"You're vapid," she snapped. "Move along or I'll call the sheriff."

"Oh, good," I said, my eyes still closed. "Could you tell him I need a ride to my house? And that Beatrice has the tea mix he ordered."

"You're disgusting, Josephine. You should really shower sometime." Her voice held a harder edge, knowing I'd bested her threat.

"Don't make me introduce you to my dog. She's infested with fleas."

I heard her move back, as the kaleidoscope of sunlight on my lids returned. Her footsteps quickly going back onto the paved path told me I'd freaked her out enough to get her to leave. "Have a nice day, Annabeth!" I called after. She might have mumbled something, but I couldn't hear it that far away.

Annabeth Montgomery came from money, and that money had been affected by us "tree huggers." More than once she'd sought me out personally to make my life harder, with snide comments and high school mean-girl tricks. I hadn't been amused. But I had found it funny to learn, after researching some family lines of my own, that hers intersected with The Row four generations back. Turns out, Miss Annabeth—with her plastic face, plastic house, and oil-guzzling car—shared the same great-grandmother as Elder Good. It made me warm inside with a smug satisfaction. It was wrong, I knew that, but it was one sick, delightful karmic splurge I tried to ignore about myself.

"I was just lying, Tater. I know you're not infested. You're a lady."

She let out a shuddering breath, rolled onto her side, and unceremoniously exposed her belly, for a rub.

"Geez, Tater, keep some mystery, for heaven's sake." She wasn't impressed and bounced side to side on her back, like only a dog could do, scratching her back.

"Okay, okay," I said, sitting up and scratching her rib cage. She let her tongue hang out. Bits of grass and soil stuck to it. "We're not disgusting. We've got character. Boys like character."

Chapter Eleven

THE RETIRED blue gate was barely standing. It had rusted through years ago and was propped onto itself. The weight pinched it together, reminding me of a saw stuck inside the trunk of a tree. Tater skirted around the side of it and bounded down the overgrown road.

"What are you feeling, Finn?" I asked as my hiking stick clicked on the gravel. He rolled a piece of cedar leaf between his fingers.

"Nothing really," he replied. "If anything did happen here, it happened quickly or farther down the trail."

I nodded and passed him, leading the way down the mucky path.

Mud pits on the trail were a great way to see what sort of animals and people had been using the trail, but the pits looked virtually untouched, except for what looked like birds and possibly a coyote or a very small dog. A coyote's paws were compact, and it would be more than exceptional to find a small dog up here without human tracks to accompany it. Tater lagged behind, smelling each stump and sniffing the new salmonberries that were brave enough to bloom early. They couldn't be her prints.

"Tater! We're working!" I called behind me and she galloped after, blasting past Finnigan and slopping through the pit. The mud splattered across the trail, up her legs, and across her belly. She was in heaven—tongue out, eyes bright—as she passed me. I felt a tug in my belly that felt like affection, and I rolled my eyes.

"What sort of mushrooms was he looking for, Swell?" Finnigan asked. "That might help us narrow down where he was headed."

"Chanterelles."

"There used to be a wonderful patch just over the ridgeline. It's been dry for a few years, but maybe he didn't know that or knew something we don't." Finnigan switched places with me, taking the lead through the underbrush as he cut upward onto a game trail. The greenery thickened, choking the path through the eerie uniformity of the tree farm planted trees. About a quarter of a mile uphill I could see an older tract of land. Large Spruce trees rose up over the canopy of alder.

The ground felt different on lumber land. It was healing and attempting to come back to its true, natural form, but there was something fractured about its energy that was raw and powerful, pooling and pocketing in distracting ways. It made most people from The Row cautious.

Tater, unaware of this energy, surfed through the ferns and salal. Her nose and tail rose over and under like a shark through waves.

"If I didn't know better," Finnigan said, "I'd say there was no way in hell he'd been able to get up here easily at his age." His breath was coming in puffs, as was mine. The terrain was steep, and it seemed unlikely Aldo would have come out here, not only because of the slope, but because chanterelles were known to pair with twenty- to thirty-year-old spruce and these were well over forty. Unlogged. Spared.

"I agree with you." I took a moment to rest, my right leg braced up the hillside and I balanced my weight with the hiking stick.

Finn crouched low to the ground, tugging at the green grass and pressing his fingertips into the soil. "But we're wrong," he said. "The trees may be older than forty, but the soil still houses the mycelium. If it had rained in the days prior to his hike, he could have hit a jackpot."

"You can feel that?" I asked, not skeptical per se, just confirming.

Finnigan mimed an offended face and pointed to himself, the cedar leaf still between his middle finger and thumb. "Plant guy. Green thumb? Planter extraordinaire?"

"Right," I said, lengthening the word and raised my eyebrows. "But remember, Beatrice still loves me the most."

"No way," he said, and we snickered.

Up ahead, Tater had stopped moving. Her body was still and her front right paw frozen in mid-step. Finnigan looked back, making eye contact with me, but no sound as he slipped into the brush on the left. I flanked Tater, approaching slowly. I projected my consciousness outward, spanning the woods in front of us for anything that could be there to make Tater go on point. My hand reached for the butt of my iron blade, the smooth handle a comfort and a strength.

The space in front of us felt empty. No deer. No squirrels. No mice. Only two birds, crows maybe, perched low to the ground thirty feet uphill. I couldn't see them, but I could feel a flittering of awareness scattered with what felt like static in the mind of a bird attracted to quick, bright, and shiny things.

Tater crouched low, slinking into the salal and over the roots that rose through a burnt-red duff. Water pooled in a spot near skunk cabbage that had just begun to grow toward the sky. Tater's body remained rigid as she moved forward with quiet attention.

Fear tingled inside my chest cavity, making the hair on the back of my neck rise. I fought the sensation as I watched Finnigan move past my side ten feet to the left. He had replaced the cedar leaf with a whittled wand of birch. His conduit of choice. Seeing his reaction and the concentration of the perpetual puppy, I realized our bodies were reacting to a predator we couldn't see.

The forest was too quiet. Too still. The sound of my heartbeat in my throat and the spruce needles under Finn's shoes sounded loud in the unnatural stillness.

Finn scanned the shrubbery and trees in front of us. Tater was no longer advancing. Her body was still once again.

With horrifying clarity, I realized we were on the perimeter of a ward. Whether it was a visual ward or one for protection, I didn't know, but we were looking directly at a glamour. Our minds perceived a benign forest in front of us, but for all we knew, an army could have been just on the other side of a thin membrane of perception.

I fought the instinct to run. Running would make me look like prey. It took great effort to keep my face and jaw relaxed, my eyebrows loose. If someone were looking at me, they would have assumed I was curious but not alarmed.

I leaned softly forward onto my hiking stick, pushing my will downward through it into the ground, sending an inquiry out through the soil. The energy moved like water. "All well?" I asked in my mind.

But the answer that came back was quick and dark, sticky. It clung to me, returning through the pathways my energy had used. It was metallic and burned the back of my mouth like a bloody nose. Dark. Tainted. Danger.

I jerked backward, my subconscious trying to shake the stink of death from my mind. It oozed toward me, attempting to breach my consciousness and press through the glamour.

Finnigan hissed as he reacted to the primal beat of the inky, dark blood magic that us. The seduction was as strong as any drug. The synapses reacting, the adrenaline, the euphoria ...

"Finnigan!" I whispered as his posture faltered and he swayed like a tree in the wind. "Finn!" He sunk to his knees, a smile touching his lips.

In order to get to him, I had to buy time. Once again, I sent my intention down through my hiking stick, pushing back against the darkness. There was a head rush of heat as I moved my spell down just below the soil and out about fifteen feet, just past Finnigan and Tater. It rose up just beyond them to create a barrier. It glimmered a light gold, reflecting like water on a pond. It hurt.

I took a deep breath and pushed the air slowly past my lips, attempting to focus the energy into a steady flow. I placed my hand onto the rough sappy bark of a nearby pine tree whose branches spread up through the canopy. "Grant me use, friend," I whispered. Its roots reached wide and its upper branches broke through the canopy as a direct source to the sky. There was a moment of pause and then a flood of reprieve. The essence of the pine smelled of sap and sunlight. It gave me the needed bump to call Tater off point and pull Finnigan away from the glamour.

He tumbled backward, end over teakettle, through the sword fern and salal. I grabbed the scruff of his leather vest and pulled. Tater growled toward the empty forest, still reacting to what couldn't be seen just past Finn's feet.

"Finn. You have to move," I said. "You're too heavy for me." His dead weight and clothes caught in the foliage making him even harder to move. "Finn!"

His eyes were glossy but he was blinking again. The darkness drained from him and time sped up with a snap. The pine had done all it could do to boost my own protection ward. "Animatus," I said. The spell tapped what was left of my already depleted energy. Finnigan jerked and sat straight up, sucking in air like he was breaking free of the ocean.

"Finnigan! You have to move!" I yelled.

He stood up, falling onto his knee once, then regained his ground. His eyes were no longer glossy, and he was Finnigan again. He shook himself like a wet dog, stood, and ran.

There was a sound of wind moving through the branches just before the trees behind us exploded, dark masses broke through the glamour and coalesced into a shape that was made of thousands of writhing winged beings.

Crows.

"Holy shit." My steps faltered.

Tater skittered toward me, spooked by the sound the wings made. Her momentum shuffled her past me. The crows were both horrific and beautiful at the same time, a solid wall of pulsing gray and blue, bobbing beaks, and claws.

Finnigan and Tater moved through the underbrush away from the liquid black swarm, but my legs refused to move. These birds didn't feel like anything I'd experienced before. All at once my shock wore off and adrenaline thrummed through me, releasing the hold gravity had on my legs. I scrambled and gained purchase on the duff, propelling myself the way we'd come, not knowing if the crows would follow and, if they did, what they could do.

I'd never been scared of a bird before, but I knew these weren't just birds. They worked together to serve a master, and that master was stronger than anyone I'd met before.

The closer we got to the blue gate, where we'd parked, the less movement I sensed behind us.

I careened over the raised embankment, sliding down on my butt after Finnigan, who had already started his truck. The driver's-side door was open and Tater safely inside the cab.

"What was that, Swell?" Finn asked. His tinged with embarrassment. "I couldn't control myself."

"Not even the strongest Magical could deny that call." I raised my free right hand and squeezed his forearm. "You're okay."

"I can still feel it." His hand raised to swipe through his hair. "I wanted to cross the glamour. I needed to."

It was quiet again around us, but I didn't trust that. For all we knew, crows could be within earshot.

"But you didn't," I said.

He nodded.

He hadn't crossed the glamour. That was true. But if I hadn't been there, Finnigan would have had no protection. He would have blissfully succumbed to the call of whatever was behind the shitstorm we had just outrun.

I squeezed Finn's arm one more time, and he squeezed

my hand in response. We touched foreheads—something we hadn't done since we were kids. "You sure can move for an old man with the right motivation," I teased.

He squeezed my hand and reluctantly laughed. The tension in his shoulders loosened. He still looked scared.

As Finn backed out of the parking spot and steered his Volkswagen toward to the main road, movement caught my eye. The hair on the back of my neck rose as a lone crow came to rest on the blue gate. Its counterpart bobbed on a nearby pine tree branch, watching.

Chapter Twelve

I WAS out of coffee and only halfway through the stack of papers Elder Todd's assistant Diedre, had dropped off this morning. They were dusty and smelled of mildew and mouse droppings.

The desk chair squeaked lightly as I shook my right leg. The spring sang and danced a high-pitched rhythm. There was a banging from next door.

"Sorry!" I called out. I always forgot about the dude next door. I leaned forward to rest my elbows on the desk, only to sneeze hard enough to shake my glasses free.

"Enough of these plague papers," I said as I stood. "I think it's time to go to The Goose for a coffee and a thick, gooey brownie."

Tater's head rose at the mention of gooey, and her tail thumped a deep bass onto the couch cushion. She jumped down and waited patiently by her leash.

"Well, aren't you manipulative," I said as I scratched her head, looped the leash around her neck, and clipped it secure. I'd trimmed her nails last night, so she was silent as she moved across the floor, but the wood floors now seemed to be ice, and she slid around a bit as we cut through the main office to the foyer and out the front door to the sidewalk.

She pranced ahead of me toward the The Spruced Goose. It was our small town's attempt at ingenuity. Half the building was a laundromat, and the other a coffee shop that made double-chocolate brownies and a killer cup of coffee. If I could, I would have it pumped directly into my veins.

Fifty feet from the shop's entrance, I could see Bronson's truck parked and idling out front. Tater could see it too, and she let out a mournful bark that sounded like a bloodhound on a scent. "Jesus," I said, trying to shrink smaller into myself. The last thing I needed was Ranger Danger asking me how I was feeling and if I had finally stopped bleeding from my eyeballs.

Tater's freshly clipped nails caught traction. She pulled me with a howl toward Bronson's truck and my inevitable humiliation. She whined, pacing back and forth between the truck and the shop's front door. Her nose left wet prints on the sidewalk.

The jangle of the bell above the shop's door announced that Bronson was returning. Instead of being pulled toward him, I instinctively dropped the leash and let Tater have her way with him.

Bronson's hair looked freshly washed—his uniform crisp and clean—and a bagel was balanced on top of his coffee cup. He didn't see her coming.

I would be lying if I said it wasn't satisfying to see sixty-five pounds of dog body-slam a man, sneak-attack style.

The bagel launched like a shot put through the air, traveling over five feet in the opposite direction of the coffee. Bronson attempted to keep the liquid inside the cup while the bagel, with cream cheese, slid to rest at my feet. But before I could stop her, Tater had snatched half of it and jumped into the open bed of Bronson's truck.

"Tater!" we said in unison.

"I'm so sorry." I scrambled to pick up the bagel that now looked like it had gathered more gravel than cream cheese. I dumbly handed it back to him. He flipped it over to see both sides, inspecting the new additions, and then searched the sidewalk for the nearest garbage can.

"Let me buy you another," I offered.

"Don't worry about it," he said as his hand rose to pat his firm stomach. "Truth be told, that was my second. I was going to take it to work with me."

"Oh." I glared at Tater, who didn't seem to think she'd created any trouble whatsoever.

"Seriously, it's fine," he said and smiled. "Don't worry. Really."

He reached out to pet Tater behind the ears. He spoke directly to her large, luminous pools of puppy eyes. "I should have just given it to you."

I smirked. "Don't encourage her. I had to move all the food to the upper cupboards this morning. You probably got the brunt of that."

"I'm just glad she's looking healthy and happy." He took ahold of Tater's leash and guided her out of the truck and onto the sidewalk.

As he smiled, his blue eyes crinkled at the corners, and I felt my hands begin to sweat. This wasn't good. I couldn't be a lumpy bag of frumpy hormones.

"Well ..." his voice trailed off. "I'll see you around, Swell."

"Okay," I said. *Okay? That's all I had to say?*

I stood frozen on the sidewalk and watched Bronson

climb into the cab of his truck, pull out onto the main road, and then turn the corner. I already wondered when I would see him next and, for God's sake, what sort of mess my heart had just stepped into.

The next day, I swung by The Spruced Goose for coffee and parked the Vanagon where Bronson's truck had been the day before. I could have made coffee at home or the office, so why was I here again? Partly, I argued, was laziness. Coffee always tasted better if someone else made it. But the other part of me worried it was because there was a possibility of running into Bronson again.

I'd left Tater with Finn today and to my surprise, I felt lonely. I'd spent the majority of my adult life working solo, and after just a few days of Tater coming to the office with me, I'd morphed into a crazy dog lady.

The Goose was popular with Ironhearts. People from The Row tended to wash and hang-dry their clothes if the weather allowed. Convenience seemed to be the Ironheart equivalent of magic. What could be better than doing two things at once—laundry and coffee—with free Wi-Fi?

I got my drink and lingered a tad longer than I needed to, adding cream and sugar while perusing the community billboard and discarded section of the local paper. There was a comforting bustle in and out of the shop that felt welcoming, and before I knew it, I had drained half the cup and started on the brownie. But Bronson never came in.

Disappointed, I walked back to the Vanagon. Beatrice's dream catcher swayed on the rearview mirror as I hoisted myself inside the cab. There was a moment of hesitation before the engine turned over. I checked my mirrors, turned on my turn signal, and pulled out into traffic toward the office.

I really didn't want to go in. It was spring, and there was a smell in the air of fresh greenery that promised long, lazy summer days ahead. There was so much to do in the garden and on Beatrice's chicken coop and goat pen. I could be doing that. The warmth of the caffeine and sugar encouraged me... *I should play hooky. Just for the day.*

I decided that once I was done with the chores, I could spend the rest of the day recuperating in the hammock under the cedar trees. Yes, that was a great plan.

I would just swing into the office, check my messages, and then slip right out. Sneaky.

I parked behind the brick building and left the coffee on the center console for good measure. I'd be right back, I reasoned.

I slipped past the empty receptionist desk and waiting area and hurried down the hall to my office. I unlocked the door, flicked on the knock-off Tiffany-style lamp in the shape of a turtle on the far wall, and with one finger, booted up the Mac.

Three new emails and a voicemail. Shit.

If I didn't read and listen to them, I would worry all day.

"Damn it," I muttered and opened the app.

Three emails were interdepartmental group notices about policy and upcoming events that were optional or required. The upcoming Solstice Celebration was required but no one would miss that. It was a blast every year and a tradition. Even people from Spruce came.

The second email was for a meeting with regional Magical councils in July that people were gearing up for and the third was a reminder to label everything in the break room fridge.

In my opinion, anyone who ate something in a Magical fridge that wasn't labeled took their life into their own hands.

I hit Reply All and typed, "How about ... If it isn't yours, don't eat it?" How about that? I hit Send. Time-stamped and proof of work.

I was almost free. I just needed to listen to the voicemail. There was a series of numbers and then a code, I had to enter to retrieve it. I was starting to regret leaving my mocha in the parking lot.

"Swell. Trigger here," the voicemail began. "I got an odd call here yesterday. Something you might want to check out. Trigger out."

Trigger was a cop with the Spruce P.D. I'd gone to high school with his older brother, who'd died overseas. I'd always thought Trigger had been nice to me because I reminded him of his brother. Occasionally, he would give me a heads-up when they got "woo-woo" calls they didn't know how to handle.

Well, shit. This was a predicament. I could pretend I hadn't heard the message and call tomorrow morning or I could take the bait. He'd never steered me wrong before.

I looked outside to the sun creeping across the tops of the Oregon grape bushes outside my window. Papers on the walls lightly rustled with the breeze. I really wanted to bail on work. I'd been so close to that afternoon hammock time.

I dialed the SPD's main line.

The phone rang three times and then a woman with a pleasant voice answered. She transferred me to Trigger's extension.

"Officer Trigger," a gruff voice answered.

He wasn't one to elaborate.

"Trigger, it's Swell. You called?"

"Heya, Swell!" His voice lifted and relaxed a bit. "Got an odd call for you."

"Okay."

"Woman up at the trailer park on Waddel Road said there were some birds bothering a neighbor. Dispatch took the message, and it was forwarded to Animal Control. But they aren't interested unless the birds are rabid or sick."

"Bothering a neighbor? What does that mean, exactly?" I leaned onto my elbows and blew steam onto the desktop. I drew a smiley face in the condensation.

"I was curious too. So I gave her a call. Woman's name is Ilene Frank." He laughed. "Real character. She said that there were crows attacking her neighbor, so she called 911."

"Okay..." I didn't see where this would be in my area of expertise.

"She said he was pretty banged up and bloody but had gotten really upset when she'd called it in."

"Ah," I said then leaned back. "Email me her address and I'll swing by."

"Will do. Take 'er easy, Swell," he said and then hung up.

A man of many words.

Chapter Thirteen

The Vanagon wasn't a fan of hills. She puttered along at a snail's pace while I roasted in the driver's seat. With all the windows down, dog hair floated like snow in the back. I'd sneezed twice just in the last mile. I could either close the windows and die of heat or sneeze up the road to the trailer park on Waddel. The road was deeply rutted gravel, which made the van shudder each time I hit a pothole. I tried to miss them but failed; the dream catcher jerked violently with each thump.

I'd worn shorts and flip-flops to the office because I really hadn't thought I'd be there long. Now, the rainbow nail polish and short-shorts didn't seem like the most professional choices. I could have gone back and changed before heading out on the lead, but I knew that I would have been too tempted to grab an iced coffee and lay out on the grass instead of being a responsible adult.

Just past the long row of mailboxes, I passed through a narrow-gated entrance and a sign that read, Hungry Hollow Trailer Estates. I snorted. That sounded horrendously bleak. In contrast, however, the majority of the trailers were new and well-maintained. Most had gardens and flowers in their front yards, and more than one sported a boat or small RV in the carport.

Aldo Fuller had also lived here. His trailer was number three and sat in stasis like a time capsule of the previous October. The carport was empty. Which was curious, since his truck had been found. I reached across the middle console to scribble a note onto an envelope on the passenger seat: "Aldo truck. Where? Find out." The blinds were all drawn, and there were several houseplants on the porch that looked healthy. It seemed someone was looking after the place.

I rolled past Aldo's and headed toward the back of the park. The call had come from Ilene Frank, who lived in space thirty-six. I took notice of which houses had kids and pets. A few had chicken coops, which I found encouraging. The house closest to Ilene's was covered on the south side with solar panels. I figured that must be the bird neighbor.

I parked behind the car in Ilene's carport. It was a sensible, dark-green Corolla. I bet it had air conditioning. I took a moment to gather myself, slung my purse across my chest, and tried to look as professional as I could in a t-shirt that had "Bigfoot Believes in You Too" printed across my chest.

Ilene seemed to like garden fans. There were several colorful fans spinning in various flower pots, as well a few porcelain yard ornaments. One was of a gnome holding a lantern and looking quite jovial. She must be an optimist, because all of our stories on The Row warned that gnomes were quite grumpy and cross.

As I climbed the steps, Ilene had her front door open and was looking at me through the screen. "You're too late!" she said. "They've gone about an hour ago."

"Mrs. Frank," I began. "I'm Josephine Swell from The

Row Council's Reconnoiter and Determinations department."

"Seems like a mouthful for someone who's a day late and a dollar short," she said through the screen. She was trying not to read my shirt.

"I apologize for the delay. I was contacted by Spruce P.D. this morning and drove right over." I tilted back onto my heels and pointed down toward my shirt. "Which gives an explanation for my casual attire."

She snorted. "You could have at least put on some pants."

"Yes, ma'am," I said, thinking maybe humility would go a ways with her.

She stepped back and opened the screen door as she did. "Come on in. Don't let the air out."

I pulled my bag closer to me and slipped inside as the screen hissed shut. I closed the thin metal trailer door behind me.

Ilene's house smelled of Pine-Sol and menthols. A stiff-looking felt couch took up a large wall of the living room, and wood shelves displayed commemorative plates and spoons of patriotic settings.

"Those are my Time Life collectibles," she said, seeing where I was looking. "I've got every one except the 9/11 plate. Didn't seem right, you know?" She was busying herself in the kitchen. "Why buy a plate to commemorate terrorists? World's gone crazy."

I heard coffee percolating.

"Markus is a computer programmer," she said as she shuffled out of the kitchen with an ashtray and a leather-pouched pack of Virginia Slims. "He lives next door." Her eyes watched me expectantly. "He's single too. Makes a nice amount of money."

I realized she was pitching the bird victim as a potential love interest for me. "I'm just here to follow up on your call."

"Oh," she said. The smile faded and her mouth pinched. "Yeah, the birds." She shook her head as she waddled over to a forest-green corduroy La-Z-Boy and sat down, expelling air like a balloon being let go. "That was the darnedest thing I'd ever seen," she said as she looked out the front bay window toward the house next door with the solar panels.

"Do you happen to know Markus's last name?" I asked.

"Wainwright," she said, lighting a long, thin cigarette. "He grew up here. His family's been here for ages. But his parents died a few years back, and now it's just him and some cousins. A nice young man." Her eyebrows raised and she smiled hopefully.

"What exactly happened with the birds?" I asked, trying to keep Ilene on task.

She took a deep breath as the cigarette burned between two fingers in her right hand. "I'm not really sure how it started. I just happened to hear some noise out front while I was doing my Tae Bo tape in the back bedroom. I came out front and saw three crows dive-bombing Markus in the road. He was swinging a newspaper at them, but they just kept going for him."

Her eyes slid back and forth as she recalled the memory.

"He was pretty banged up and screaming about them not getting him. When he saw me come out onto the porch, he told me to go back inside. So I did." She puffed on her cigarette, which glowed, releasing a vapor of smoke toward the textured ceiling.

"I called 911, but of course no one came. But I did receive a phone call," she said with a laugh. "What good does a phone call do?" She shook her head. "This afternoon, before you came, I saw Markus pull out of his driveway. And I'll be damned if those crows weren't waiting for him. One was even on his windshield wiper, bobbing up and down."

"It was on his car?" I asked, startled.

"Oh yes!" she said, "The wipers were even on, and they were swinging away with a crow on it. The other two were circling above the car as he drove away."

"They followed the car?" This was getting interesting.

"Yes and they never made a sound."

I'm not sure how long I sat in Mrs. Frank's driveway, but it was long enough to cause her to pull her curtains partially open and peer out. I waved, what I hoped was reassuringly, and tried to make it look like I was on the phone. In reality, I was trying not to freak out. Something felt very bad and very wrong about all of this. I can handle teenagers on The Row daring each other to try out a dark magic spell, or the rare revenge spell by a jilted lover but dealing with someone who's able to summon Elementals and alter animal behavior was completely different.

I worried my thumb's cuticle until I could feel a piece of skin pull up, and I bit it off.

I called into the office and left a voicemail at the desk for an inquiry into Markus Wainwright. I was looking specifically for a current phone number and any friends or family he might have in the area. Mrs. Frank had said that his parents were gone, but that didn't mean he didn't have any aunts or uncles. Plus, it wouldn't be the first time a nosy neighbor had been misled.

I realized then that I'd been in the driveway for too long, so I backed out of the drive and parked on the street. Once I had finished off the coffee, I walked over to Markus's trailer. It was slate gray with blue shutters. All the blinds were closed. A quick walk around the front of the building let me know he didn't own a lawn mower. The majority of his yard was gravel, but growing in that gravel were very rare and unique succulents. They were quite impressive.

I slipped through the empty carport and went through the gated fence into the backyard was shocked to find a well-established garden. The soil in the bed was dark and rich. There was a cold frame leaned up against the backyard shed, with potatoes and onions growing up and out of the frame. *In May?* There was also a simple greenhouse framed out that was halfway finished. It seemed that Markus had an unusually green thumb. I had a feeling that he had probably been the one taking care of Aldo's houseplants. There was a tingle of connection in my brain. The sooner I got ahold of Markus, the better.

When I exited the gate, I saw Mrs. Frank get into her car and back out of the driveway, cigarette still in hand and menthol smoke trailing behind as she drove away.

Chapter Fourteen

Markus Wainwright stood tucked into the shadows at the corner of Spruce and Pine Streets. There were no birds here, at least from what he could tell.

He'd driven to the public parking garage and slipped his car into a spot on the bottom floor. The birds hadn't followed him to the lower level. It had been the first time in a week that he had been alone. But he couldn't help but feel it was only a matter of time before the crows gathered enough courage to venture down to the sub-basement level to find out what he was doing. He'd stayed inside his car for a few moments, allowing himself to soak in the stillness that wasn't tainted by crows silently watching nearby. Eventually he pulled together his messenger bag and slung it over his shoulder, took a deep breath, and braced himself for the three-block dash to The Row's Council office.

He looked down the roadway, searching for the quickest but safest way to move along the edges of the buildings where crows circling above or sitting in trees would easily miss him. There was a path in shade across Pine Street toward the office, but it would lead him directly into the park at the center of town. If he attracted attention from above, his mind reasoned, he'd be close enough to the office that he could still reach it.

It was as good a time as any. He pulled the messenger bag closer, looked up to a clear sky, and ran.

The metal clasps on the bag's straps jangled, and his footfalls jarred inside his head. The beats of his heart in his neck and the sound of his lungs pulling air into his out-of-shape body seemed to be excruciatingly loud. Those little bastards weren't stupid. They were looking for him—he knew it—and any sound could pull their attention.

The end of the shaded area between Pine and Oak Streets was coming to an end and the bright, sunbaked blacktop that separated him from the park and the office was as foreboding as a lava bed. He rededicated himself to his mission, looked both ways), and barreled forward into the sun toward the park.

He was halfway across the street when a cold jab of fear cut through his adrenaline. His shadow wasn't alone on the roadway. Three moving silhouettes arched across his own.

The airborne shapes circled above in a demented figure eight, silently. If he hadn't looked down, he would never have known they were there. He broke through to the cover of the oak trees, knowing that the crows were above him in the canopy. Fifteen feet remained to the road and then twenty-five feet to the office.

He jerked sideways as a small but solid bird body made contact with the back of his head. Markus stumbled onto one knee. The rough path ripped a hole in his pants. He stood up, startled by the pain, realizing he had cut open his knee. It was too late now. He had to finish the job. He clutched the bag closer to his body and stepped directly into the path of Ilene Frank's sensible Toyota Corolla.

Abigail's room was small, cozy, and decorated with soft comforters, pink pillows, and pictures of smiling faces. She had surrounded herself with pictures of dances, Friday-night games, cheerleading, community garden work, and church activities.

"She was a good girl," Rebecca, Abigail's mother, said from the door, arms wrapped around her small frame. "She didn't sneak out. She didn't need to." Her voice was quiet but strong.

"Did she have a boyfriend?"

"No."

"Sometimes..." I began.

"No," Rebecca insisted.

"It looks like she was very active in the community," I said, pointing to the pictures and awards on the walls.

Rebecca nodded, still just outside the doorframe. "She loved helping people, loved animals. I had to make sure she wasn't volunteering too much. And now..." Her voice trailed off, eyes seeing something in her mind.

"And now?" I pressed gently. I waited while she processed her grief. I didn't want to touch anything. Moving anything felt like a violation of Abigail's privacy, but now I supposed it was of her memory.

Rebecca picked up a small bear from the end of the bed and squeezed it to her chest. "She had stuffed animals still for Christ's sake, and for people to say she was looking for trouble ..."

I sighed and shifted my weight. The floorboard groaned slightly under me.

My mother had been slandered too. People had said she'd deserved what happened to her. That her low morals and magic had made her an easy and obvious target. That she was a slut.

"I'm so sorry, Mrs. Steele. That's not right for them to say."

"I knew your mother, you know," she said, fiddling with the ear of the bear. She sighed and set it back down on the bed.

I was skewered to the floor, wanting to know more but also afraid. No one had spoken about my mother after the rumors had circulated.

"She wasn't what they made her out to be, and I'd said nothing," Rebecca said, wiping her face with both hands.

"That wasn't your fault and neither is ..." I said. "Abigail was a good person. She didn't deserve what happened. No one does."

She gulped a sob.

"Was there anything out of the ordinary leading up to the day Abigail was found? Had she been tense or moody? Sad, maybe?" I asked.

"No." Rebecca shrunk into herself, shadows forming around her eyes. "Andrew was working, I was working. The kids had school and practices and volunteering. Everything was normal." She began to cry. "Now nothing is normal."

She's wasn't wrong,

"Abigail wouldn't have gone into the woods alone," Rebecca continued. "I mean, birds creeped her out, for God's sake. Why would she go alone?"

"Birds?" I asked.

Rebecca nodded. "She'd said there were some sick crows in the woods out back a few weeks ago. She didn't want to go out and feed the goats without someone coming with her. So why would she go out at night, alone, in the dark?"

Chapter Fifteen

I COULD FEEL the summer coming. It created a stir of creativity and joy in most of us on The Row. It was hard to stay asleep for me this time of year—especially after tossing and turning for two agonizing hours, bent in awkward angles around a dog (who took up more bed than I did).

There was a puzzle shuffling around in my head. I knew I was missing something, and if I could fit something—even a tiny piece—then I might be able to move forward with the missing person's case. I needed to find Markus Wainwright to ask him some questions, and maybe be able to make a connection to the Blood Magic used to murder Abigail Steele.

Could there be a connection between all three? I couldn't help but notice a theme poking through the details. The crows where Aldo had gone missing, the three crows that had been bothering Markus, and the single black feather that had rested on Abigail's body when she'd been found.

It all stunk of malice.

I slipped out of bed and placed bare feet to worn wood.

I grabbed my gardening sweater from behind the captain's chair at the top of the stairs and slid it on over my head. It smelled of fresh air and lilacs. Like spring.

I knew the only way I would be able to fall asleep was to make a strong pot of coffee and bake some cookies. I padded down the stairs to the dark landing next to Beatrice's pottery studio and headed toward the kitchen.

I used my fingers against the hallway wall to guide me, eyes wide open to let in any ambient light. I loved living here; the oil lamps, the wood smoke rising up from the houses tucked below the trees, and the comfort. A tender feeling pulled in my chest.

I moved barefoot across smooth, uneven, wood plank flooring to a thick, colorful hooked rug that spread between the main kitchen island and the kitchen sink. I could still remember the feel of the fabric ripping between my fingers as we took old t-shirts, pillowcases, and sheets to create material to make the rug with. As a kid, it had been a bore but looking back now as an adult, it felt fonder. My toes squeezed into the rug as I rocked from heel to toe to reach up for ingredients in the various cupboards. The mixing bowls were below the counter, and the chocolate chips were hidden on the top shelf between the oven and the sink. I used the term "hidden" loosely. I knew they were there because I'd stashed them like a miner hid their gold. I didn't share chocolate so well.

By the time I had the majority of ingredients mixed into a large metal bowl, I heard movement upstairs coming from Finn's room. It seemed he was having a hard time sleeping too. But he'd definitely picked a convenient time to come down.

"Couldn't sleep?" he asked as he pulled on a well-used t-shirt.

I nodded and stirred in the last of the chocolate chips and cleaned the spatula off, letting a glob of cookie dough drop into the bowl. "If you help me scoop these onto the tray, I'll let you have the spoons."

Finn raised his eyebrows and smiled. "Deal!" He opened the draw below the counter to grab four spoons and began to scoop and scoot the dough into uneven mounds onto the tray.

We took turns emptying the bowl onto two trays, and as the cookies baked, we played a game of rummy with cards older than we were.

"Remember the time Beatrice had us help restore the spring above Spruce?" I asked.

Finn scrunched his brows. "Yeah... What made you think of that?"

"I took a run along the ridgeline a couple days ago and ended up sitting on the outcropping above it." I played a set of three queens and discarded a three of clubs. "It seems like just yesterday that we were kids, and now we're supposed to be the adults." I took a drink of my iced coffee, the ice cubes rattling in the glass.

"You can't stop time," Finn said.

I snorted. "Thanks, Finn." He played a queen on my set and discarded a seven of clubs. "Do you ever think about Mom?" I asked.

He watched me draw a card and shuffle it among the cards in my hand. "Only when it rains."

"So almost every day." My memories of her were foggier than his. I only remembered snippets of her; her blond hair, the smell of jasmine, and her laugh. Her laugh had been contagious.

"What about you?" he asked.

I discarded a six of clubs. "Just when I'm breathing."

The cookies were getting close to done in the oven. The rich, sweet, smell of chocolate and vanilla radiated in the cozy atmosphere. It was just about that time that Tater made an appearance, loping down the steps from my room, to plop down on the rug near the sink.

"Glad you could join us," I said. Her thumping tail said she was glad also.

Once the cookies had cooled enough, I scooped them onto a cooling rack and broke a mangled, super-hot cookie in half to share with Finn. He flipped his hand of cards over face down onto the table and took the cookie chunk, popping it entirely into his mouth. "What's going on with you and that ranger?" He blew out his mouth to cool the burning-hot cookie magma in his mouth.

"Nothing."

"You sure?"

"Get your mind out of the gutter and finish the game."

He smiled. "Swell and Bronson sitting in a tree, K.I.S.S..."

"Finish that phrase, and a burnt tongue will feel like a hug." I drew from the discard pile up to the three of clubs, set down a run of clubs from the three to the eight and discarded a Jack of Hearts. "Rummy!"

"No way! Finn said. "You cheated!"

"You're just a sore loser." I grabbed another cookie and took a bite. "Help me finish these dishes."

"Sorry, Sis." He snagged a cookie, then two more. "Super tired. Gotta hit the hay."

"Oh my God."

"Night!" he called over his shoulder as Tater followed close behind.

I smiled after him.

I didn't want to think about what was or wasn't

happening with Ranger Danger. I kept making a fool of myself, and he wasn't a part of my life on The Row. It wasn't easy for an Ironheart to understand my need to stay here, to be close to the land. I didn't think I could bring myself to explain to someone new why I would always choose my family over a money and land over a career. I was the land and it was me. It couldn't be separated or undone.

I put away the cooled cookies in the bread pantry and wiped the crumbs into the sink. I placed the dirty dishes on the counter to the right of the sink and began to methodically work my way through them. When each was clean, I set them onto the counter upside down to dry.

It was getting well into the early morning hours, and I knew I should get to sleep, but I was still wide awake and buzzing with the expectation of the Solstice and the summer ahead. The death of Abigail Steele, the glamour of crows, and the summoning of Elementals were also buzzing back and forth inside my head, fighting for attention.

I sighed and decided to double down, pouring another cup of coffee. I grabbed the shawl from the back of the living room couch and settled in to make the most of my insomnia by reading files I'd brought home from the office. They all seemed pretty mundane, annotated with jargon I wasn't familiar with. Family histories from both Spruce and The Row were organized into lists and pinwheels. Names were marked with affinities for specific types of magic. In many cases, the same magic (or lack of) would follow an entire line from great-great-grandmother to great-great-grandchild.

Two names mingled back and forth between the lists; Montgomery and Good. And in one file—so old only the dust held it together—a notation of "(E.A.)" marked the eldest daughter of Annabeth Montgomery's great-great-

great-grandmother's line. I doubted it stood for "evil incarnate," but I smiled nonetheless. Notations like these didn't always indicate magic but could reveal occupations or political affiliation.

Somewhere along the way, Tater came back down from Finn's room (probably after his cookies had run out) and jumped up to curl next to me on the couch. Her big brown eyes were offset by eyebrows that showed worry.

"Go to sleep, Tater," I said. She shifted her eyebrows right to left. "I'll wake you up in a bit, when I go back to bed." She pondered this for a moment, then shuddered a sigh and passed straight out. I quickly followed her lead.

Chapter Sixteen

An email from Diedre came in around noon to let me know that SPD was now finished with the Abigail Steele crime scene and it was being released to me for decontamination. I felt an urgency to get there and make sure that there was no debris or crime scene tape left behind, so that no one would suspect something dark to have occurred there. But I also felt sadness and regret about erasing the signs of death that would also wipe clean someone's last moments.

It felt very final.

I sat at my desk, staring at the office phone for a full ten minutes while picking at my cuticles. I'd cleaned dark magic before but this was different. I needed an anchor that wasn't vulnerable to the intoxicating effects of blood magic. I couldn't go alone, and I couldn't bring someone from The Row or even the Council. An Ironheart could work, but they would be still bound by any natural laws, a spell could always affect them.

I argued with myself back and forth as to why I was even considering calling Ranger Danger. To be fair, the scene was in his park. In theory, I only needed to let him know when I was successful at removing the imprint of blood magic. But no one from The Row could be fully trusted alone with the lure of such strong magic, including myself. I couldn't help but remember the look on Finn's face as he had responded to the glamour. I'd felt it too—the hum of excitement, the pull of mystery, the thrill of discovery but I'd also felt the potential for regret, and danger.

This brought the image of Bronson to mind. My gut told me what had happened at the base of the Elementals was important. There was a reason the summoning spell had fried me in an instant but moved around Bronson, like water around a rock in a river. I needed him to have my back even if he was annoying as hell. I also tried to ignore the butterflies in my stomach that flittered as I picked up the phone and dialed the ranger station's dispatch number.

THE PARKING LOT WAS MUCH FULLER THIS TIME AS I stopped the van a good two hundred feet from the embankment down to the river. I cracked the two front windows open and distracted Tater with hashbrowns from The Spruced Goose. I jumped out and locked her in, wanting to keep her at a safe distance just in case anything went wrong.

Scanning the cars in the lot, it appeared Bronson wasn't here yet. But once his truck drew near, Tater's tail thumped against the inside of the van's sliding door like a bass drum.

"Now, don't you be getting a crush," I told her. "Ironhearts don't stick around the likes of us." Her head tilted to the side, but her tail continued to wag.

I'd changed twice; once to look less childish and the second time to look more like me. I'd settled on a neon-green t-shirt under my thick, charcoal-colored wool jacket with the copper clasps, and black jeans that I shoved into mid-calf-high boots. I hoped the jeans looked semi-professional because I sure as hell wasn't going to wear slacks. Who would wear slacks into the woods?

Bronson parked next to me and exited with a shit-eating grin. "Great to see you, Swell," he said as he pulled his state-issued ranger jacket from behind the truck's bench seat. "I was surprised to hear from you."

"Yeah, well..." I tried to sound like it was my decision. "I found that an outside assistant in this situation would be beneficial."

"Assistant?" His eyebrows rose. Not in surprise but in delight.

"It seems the magic here, on your land, and where Aldo Fuller's truck was found is a tad stronger than most can resist. You're here to make sure I don't go all black eyes and bloody again."

He nodded. "That would be best."

"Indeed." I grabbed my hiking stick and proceeded across the lot to the faint trail down from the pavement. I didn't ask him to follow me. I thought he'd get too much satisfaction from that, and try as I might, I didn't feel the home-court advantage when Ranger Danger was involved.

"Speaking of Aldo Fuller," I said as I navigated the ferns and roots at my feet. "Do you happen to have his truck at impound?"

"I did." He barely made a sound behind me. "But it was released back to the family."

"Family?" I stopped to look back at him. "The file didn't say he had family."

"Oh, he does. Cousins twice removed on both sides."

"Well, who picked it up?" I was excited because it was the first real lead I'd had.

"The Montgomerys." He moved around me to go down the trail first.

"As in Annabeth Montgomery? Hoity-toity Annabeth Montgomery is related to Aldo Fuller?"

He nodded, not looking back. "She surely is. THE Annabeth Montgomery is related, not only to Aldo Fuller, but to a specific ranger as well. Not to mention some cousins on the Wainwright side."

Holy shit. "Wait... You're related to two out of the three people I'm investigating right now, and you didn't think to mention it?"

"You didn't ask."

I closed my eyes, letting the sound of the nearby water and birds wash away the anger I was feeling. If I wasn't in the right frame of mind, I wouldn't be able to do my job. Magic was specific like that. Say what you mean, but feel what you say, and all that. Blood magic was naturally resistant to anything that could disperse it. I couldn't afford to be distracted, because I only had one shot. Besides being dangerous, Blood Magic was smart. It could retain new information. It remembered people and it learned their behavior. I had just one chance to use my ability before it blocked me out. It was similar to how the body would remember a threat to its immune system by flooding the body with antibodies to rid the immune system of disease.

I didn't want to be the disease, it knew how to defend itself from.

"Everything all right?" Bronson asked.

"You know what? Maybe it's better if we don't speak."

"Suit yourself."

I proceeded down to the small clearing that was oddly void of leaves and debris.

"They must have taken it for trace." Bronson's voice was closer than I'd expected.

"That's not how this works." I was irritated. "That trace," I snapped, "is still contaminated." I pushed a thick section of hair that had worked loose from my braid, behind my ear. "God knows where it is now."

I crouched down, careful not to touch anything but the soles of my shoes and the bottom of my hiking stick to the ground. I could still do the spell, of course, but I'd have to follow up with Trigger at the SPD, as to where the contaminated evidence had gone.

"You should probably take a few steps back," I said, looking up. "I would go a good three feet into the leaves if I were you."

He seemed to gauge the truthfulness of what I was saying and then nodded moving through last fall's crisp leaves. He stopped next to a tall hemlock that was more than four feet from the perimeter and crossed his arms across his chest.

I took a deep breath in through my nose and slowly emptied it through my mouth, imagining blowing it through a straw. I repeated this, becoming more aware of my breath, my body, and my place within the area—one foot out, two, five, ten feet on both sides—which was almost to the barrier I'd imagined. Just short of where Bronson stood next to the tree.

Twenty feet across wasn't enough room. I pressed out a foot farther on either side of me, feeling the invisible membrane of the Blood Magic resist, then sink into my barrier.

I felt cotton against my cheeks and the smell of warm, freshly dried laundry. I could feel the essence of Abigail.

I would like to say that whatever had happened here had been fast, but that wasn't true. There was pain here. A lingering. It was as if the caster had waited to let the victim ripen like a farmer does their crops.

She had bled out slowly, the fear magnifying the spell.

I felt a heavy sadness.

Chapter Seventeen

BRONSON WATCHED Swell as she took stock of the area around her. The thick wool of her jacket lightly brushed the ground as she kneeled to rest knees and shins flat to the ground. With her hiking stick she drew a circle in the soil around her. Next, she pulled four different stones from her coat pocket and placed one at each directional location, all the while her eyes remained closed.

She spoke softly, her voice too light to be carried by the breeze to his ears. He watched intently as the area within the clearing begin to change.

Cyclical segments surrounded Swell, moving as a viscous globe of texture. Segments of awareness rose and fell like water at varying speeds. The trees bent slightly inward toward Swell, whose head tilted forward. A lock of thick, dark hair escaped her braid, and it moved in space around her.

Though her eyes were closed, Bronson knew Swell could see more than he could. As she continued to speak, a pressure began to build inside him. He wanted to enter the circle even though he'd been told to stay back.

She stood with an unnaturally slow speed to turn counterclockwise from the northern position to face west. The trees and bushes made a slow rustle, like a sigh, as air moved past them in a vacuum. All at once the colors within the clearing changed. Before Bronson's eyes, the trees, soil, bushes, and air processed and recycled their nutrients, shimmering and spinning; a pixilation in the anti-gravity of space.

Rainwater rippled up from the ground. It levitated inches from and sparkled like diamond snow. Buds that had been breaking clear of limbs and the thick, green undergrowth in the approach of spring shrank downward to stand dormant for the unnatural winter.

Now that she was facing south, Bronson could only see Swell in profile, but he knew the spell continued as the leaves and berries on the limbs and vines around her bloomed in reverse. What leaves remained on the ground tipped upward, spinning like tops as they rose to rest on the branches they had fallen from. The leaves were more supple and pliant as they rose, first yellow, then orange, then a rich, bright green.

Bronson was caught by the sensuality of the ritual. The slow, methodical movement. The color in Swell's cheeks and the flush of his own. Once again, Swell turned counterclockwise to face him. Late summer winds spun within the clearing. Delicate parasols of yarrow pushed up from the ground and released their tiny petals to the wind. Swell's eyes opened, but they didn't see Bronson; the pupils remained fully dilated, and her breath was long and deep. She was getting tired as she pulled the will to finish from the earth around her.

Though outside the barrier, Bronson could smell the warm scents of late summer, and it made his heart ache for sunshine. Swell's mouth parted open, suspended mid-breath. Her head dropped back, bringing Bronson to awareness that the spell sat on the verge of overpowering her. Swell would never have wanted him to see her this way, in such a personal moment. He argued to himself that what she was doing was her job and a normal part of the process. He wasn't intruding. But the quickness of his heartbeat and the heat in his mouth told him he was lying to himself.

Swell moved to face north. The wind and rain slowed, and leaves of various colors fluttered down from the branches. She returned to rest on her knees and laid the hiking stick on a bed of freshly sprouted green grass. Still quietly casting, she raised both of her arms up as Bronson vaguely recognized a flash of metal before a familiar blade swung down to Swell's open hand. A line of red bubbled up, and she rested both hands facedown to the soil and cried.

Without thinking, he stepped through the barrier. "Are you okay?" he asked, crossing the clearing in four steps.

Swell, still kneeling on all fours, turned her head to look up at him. "Who the fuck kills a kid?" She gulped a wracking sob, and he tried to comfort her by rubbing her back until finally she grew quiet.

Chapter Eighteen

"Don't touch the stones," I said, trying not to puke. I could not let myself toss the lunch of cupcakes, which I'd eaten on the way to the park, in front of Ranger Danger.

"Do we wait?" he asked. He wasn't rubbing my back anymore, but he was still too close for comfort.

"No. The rocks stay here." I wrapped my hand with the fabric I had tucked into my pocket. It wasn't bleeding anymore, but it stung like hell. "They've still got some mojo in case the spell didn't work."

"Oh, it worked," he said.

I raised my eyebrows and forced myself to stand. I thought the cleaning had worked too, mostly because it felt like I had the worst hangover of my life.

I usually felt tired after I worked with Blood Magics. I would need chocolate and coffee through an IV drip before I would be able to fully open my eyes, without the hammering headache I felt coming.

"Was that normal?" Bronson asked.

"Was what normal?" I used my good hand to brush the dirt and leaves from my clothes.

"The cutting, bleeding, crying parts."

I sighed. "Honestly, no."

Nothing felt normal.

"Unlike Ironhearts," I said, "we can't take from the earth without maintaining a balance. We don't consider trees and soil a resource. They're our equals." I straightened. "What you saw wasn't Blood Magic, but an offering to keep that balance."

All of that was true, but I didn't want to tell Bronson that the Blood Magic I had just scrubbed from the ground had been a completely different beast. It was stronger, unpredictable, and had taken more out of me than any other cleaning before.

I moved past Bronson and scaled the trail to the parking lot, where a silhouette of Tater paced back and forth inside the Vanagon. I unlocked the door and slid it open. She to licked my arms and face. "I'm okay, Tater." I tried to calm her, but she knew I was full of it.

"Oh, Jesus! Tater, stop!" I pushed her back and rested the hiking stick on the floor of the van.

It took me a second to register the sound of the driver's side door opening and Bronson sliding in. My mouth fell open. "What are you doing?" I stammered. "Get out of the van!" I leaned against doorframe for support.

"You need coffee," he said, turning from the steering wheel to face me.

"I'm fine." I did want coffee though. I weighed my options.

He smiled. "My treat." He was baiting me. I knew it and there was no way I could drive.

"You're buying me a brownie too," I said. Tater whined from the back, her swinging tail caused the van to sway slightly. "And something for Tater."

Ranger Danger pondered this for a moment, then broke into a toothy grin. "Deal!"

Shit.

I TRIED NOT TO LOOK AT BRONSON BENT BEHIND THE wheel of Beatrice's Volkswagen. I didn't want to see him looking adorably comfortable in any aspect of my life. Though I'd resisted growing attached to Tater, I felt the twinge of jealousy as she looked at him with those huge eyes, tail wagging, like he'd hung the moon.

I mean, I'd just turned back time in a spell bubble. Where was my adoration?

At least I'd be getting caffeine and sugar out of this mess.

I finally dared to steal a glance at Bronson. "Why didn't you get hurt?" I asked. It was the question that had bothered me, one that I'd been afraid to ask.

"Hmm?" His right eyebrow rose in question as he turned his head from the road to look my way.

"Why didn't you get hurt?" I carefully enunciated each word so he could hear them over the engine. "Why did I get fried alive and you looked like a Robert Redford stunt double? It parted around you. I saw it."

He shrugged. One tanned hand gripped the steering wheel while the other tapped on the bottom of the wheel. "I honestly don't know." His dark-brown hair moved in the wind that blew in through the cracked window.

Tater had finagled her way between the front seats and rested her head onto his leg.

I couldn't believe that. I looked away. Ironhearts weren't immune to magic. No one was.

There could have been a past blood protection spell done on his family line that moved the blast of spell around him or his blood specifically altered the original ward and triggered a new reaction. But even then he would have had some sort of interaction with it. His hair hadn't even moved.

The spell could have been set for me, but that was unlikely as there was no way anyone could have predicted I would be there to trigger it.

I would need to go back to Bronson's property and try to find out who had set the spell. And that wasn't a pleasant thought. My nose began to vibrate with the memory of the blood that had spurted from it when the concussion of the spell had hit me. I could have drowned in my own blood if Bronson hadn't somehow released me from the ward barrier. And how had that worked? It defied everything I knew about magic.

The van rumbled down the mountain toward Spruce. Two blocks from town square a large group of people blocked Main Street with signs and banners. Their clothes were bright and layered, and their heads crowned with knit caps. "What fresh hell is this?" I asked.

"Someone must have tipped off the activists that the lumber company is planning on logging the stand of trees just above the park," Bronson said. His face showed no emotion.

"They're planning to log what?" I almost came out of my seat, rising and turning to face him. "Why would they be logging that? It's only thirty years old!" I felt like I'd been hit in the gut. The Row Council was negotiating a sale, to buy that tract. The profit from the sale would be more than the lumber company would have gotten for the lumber, and traditionally they didn't harvest until the trees had reached at least forty years old.

"How long have you known about this?" I asked. I wanted to take it out on him for knowing and not saying anything.

"Since the day we brought your buddies Larry and Frank in."

The fucking poachers.

I hadn't made the connection that they were logging so close to The Row. The Council would be upset when they heard.

Maybe they already knew.

The Row Council's top priority should have been to protect and conserve land, especially land that had already been abused enough by the lumber practices.

"Don't you people ever learn?" I crossed my arms and looked forward. "Lumber isn't an industry that will bring prosperity. Your own practices collapsed the industry."

"Whoa," Bronson said, then pulled the van over. "They weren't MY practices, all right? I might be from a logging family, but I didn't single-handedly destroy this town and create years of poverty. So get that straight." He turned off the ignition, opened the driver's-side door, and climbed out.

Now I wouldn't get that coffee. But that wasn't my only fear. I'd offended him, and I hadn't meant to. "Bronson. I'm sorry." The words tumbled out of my mouth. "I didn't mean you, you. I meant Ironhearts and even then, I should have kept my mouth shut." I looked him in the eye. "I apologize."

Tater whined between us, and I scratched behind her ears.

He leaned against the van's door frame, the color of his uniform making the green of his eyes stand out. Small flecks of orange floated in them. With a sigh, he pushed off the van and said, "Let's get you that coffee. We might be able to find a brownie."

"Oh, thank God," I said, clipping Tater's leash to the back of her harness. I opened the passenger door, letting her hop through the front seat. We joined Bronson at the front of the van and headed toward the moving crowd that rolled with flags and drums.

Chapter Nineteen

THE PROTESTORS HAD DONE a great job of blocking the road and sidewalk between our parking spot and The Goose. The faces in the crowd weren't familiar and most seemed very young. I didn't want to be cynical, but through experience I knew it took a lot of naivete to take on a lumber company. To do it, you either needed to be extremely pissed or ignorant to take on the task.

Signs rose above the heads and drumbeats. "Stop Logging!" one sign read. Another seemed to scream in bold red letters, "Protect Our Mother! Save the Trees!" But my favorite was an obnoxiously large white sign with bold blue letters that read, "Down the Giants! Call Timber to Capitalism!"

Most people didn't know that New York corporations owned the largest percentage of private land in the United States. What they logged didn't affect them personally. Their "holdings" were abstract investments they doomed for harvest without ever setting foot in the woods they logged.

I pulled my wool coat closer to my frame and let Tater

pull on the leash to guide me through the crush of the crowd. Once we broke through, I noticed that Bronson was talking to one of the female protesters, who definitely was not an Ironheart. She stood a lithe five foot seven-ish and was covered in leathers and fur. Thick curls of dark brown, blue, and burgundy hair framed her face and billowed down her back. She looked like a modern goddess of the hunt. I tried to ignore the odd sensation in my belly that roiled like a snake.

Bronson smiled openly. The corners of his eyes crinkled as he raised his arms wide and fully hugged the woman, who raised her arms to hug him back.

Tater whined at my feet while we waited just off the road, near a newspaper box. I scratched her absently behind the ear while I watched them interact. They spoke animatedly and Bronson broke into a full gut laugh. They hugged one more time and broke apart, each heading in a different direction. The Magical woman moved toward the front of the protest while Bronson moved toward us.

"Old friend?" I asked, trying to seem passively interested.

He smiled and ran one hand through his hair. "Something like that." He shifted his weight on the balls of his feet. "We went to university together."

"University?" My eyebrows rose. "That's a pretty fancy term."

"Yeah..." He smirked, turning to clearly evade my questions. "You ready for that coffee?"

He might not have wanted to answer my questions, but my curiosity—and maybe some jealousy—had been roused. It was very rare for Magicals to go to college, let alone work within Ironheart movements. It also hinted that Bronson knew more about magic than I'd given him credit for.

I tied Tater up just outside The Goose's entrance. The leash laid slack on the sidewalk. The wooden signpost would be no match for her, if she decided she wanted to do something other than wait, but she sat patiently after she huffed and eased to the ground. I was uncomfortable leaving her out there and the significance of that wasn't lost on me.

The frankenshop definitely had more business than usual this time of day, and I attributed that to the demonstration outside. Most of the families in Spruce came from or were directly linked to logging. So this issue was a double-edged sword. Some would think that logging that tract of land could help them get out of a financial hole—that it would be "the answer" to all their problems. The others would realize that the tract was an answer to a month of bills, at most.

It didn't matter what side of the issue you were on. Sprucers were stirring with the influx of strangers and the protest had them buzzing.

Bronson was true to his word, getting me an iced white-chocolate americano and a hefty chocolate brownie. "As advertised," he said, leading me to the last open window seat. He went back for a cute little pot of loose leaf tea and a scone.

"That isn't exactly what I expected you to get," I said. I never would have pegged him for the herbal tea sort.

"What did you expect me to get?"

"I don't know... Slim Jims and a bucket of cowboy coffee?" I said and took a bite of the brownie.

He snorted. "I've never been able to drink coffee, but I got into the habit of tea in college and it stuck."

I took a larger bite of brownie and washed it down with ice-cold coffee, stealing a peek at Tater, who was happily taking up the majority of sidewalk in front of the shop. She was still looking toward the group of people, her wet nose pausing for a moment and then twitching with each inquisitive sniff. She was having a blast.

"You said *university* before..." I paused for another sip of coffee. "Does that mean you went to school outside the States? It's a pretty European term."

He corralled some crumbs on the black tabletop, scooped them into his hand, and brushed them onto his plate. "I went to college in Canada. Montreal, to be exact." He leaned back and turned his teacup counterclockwise. "And full disclosure, I also speak French. So ..." His voice trailed off.

"So?"

"I can arrest you in at least two languages."

"Be still my heart." I laughed. "I guess in the spirit of full disclosure," I said, air-quoting the last two words, "I should tell you that I've felt better for about twenty minutes. But since I had you on the hook for caffeine and sugar, I wasn't going to let that go to waste."

He smiled then took another sip of tea. "Noted." Bronson leaned back, looking at his watch, and sucked in a breath. "Oh! I've gotta get back to work." He pushed back his chair and stood up. "I'm sorry, but I've got to get going. You're all paid. And these," he said, putting Beatrice's keys in front of me on the table, "are yours."

"Oh," I said dumbly, beginning to stand. "I can drive you."

"No worries." He waved my offer away. "Samantha's going back that way and offered to give me a ride."

'Oh." I was surprised. He was already looking out the window to where I could now see his friend waiting. "Okay.

Well, thanks for ..." I paused awkwardly. "Er, um, everything."

"Not a problem! Take care." He thanked the girl behind the counter as he passed and was gone in a flash, leaving the smell of juniper and sage after him. I remained sitting, feeling confused and startled as he patted Tater goodbye and darted across the street.

Samantha's face lit up as he approached. Her gaze swung to where I sat in the shop's window.

How the hell can someone covered in death-fashion look delicate? I sighed.

I must have looked how I felt, because before I knew it, Annabeth Montgomery pounced on me like a leopard on a wounded gazelle. "You know, I never thought I'd say this," she leaned in smelling of expensive perfume, bracelets jangling as loudly as her yellow polka dot dress, "But you're definitely not as disgusting as her." She grinned. "And that's something, right?"

"Go away." I gathered my purse and coffee; wrapping the remaining portion of the brownie in a napkin. I just wanted to get out of there. I could feel my face burning and Annabeth was the last person I wanted to witness it.

I got halfway to the door before I decided to take out my embarrassment on someone other than myself. "I bet these protestors put a crimp in your cash flow, huh?" I snapped at Annabeth.

But she surprised me.

"My family isn't logging anything. We haven't logged in over two years. But you wouldn't know that since you were in the big city breaking hearts." She pushed the sleeves of her cardigan up. "We haven't logged since my father's company was bought out by Mark's company."

"Mark's company?" I didn't understand and I didn't want to think about him.

I was surprised to see Annabeth hesitate. "I'm sorry. I thought you knew."

"Knew what?"

"The company Mark works for bought out my father. Over two years ago. Mark runs their forestry department now."

I felt like I had been punched in the gut. I thought my split with Mark had been amicable… "healthy." All the words that described a conscious "un-coupling," as the celebrities called it these days. But to find out that my ex-fiancé hadn't given me a heads-up on a pivotal timber harvest made me wonder if he'd kept other information from me when we were together. And to hear it from Annabeth… It really pissed me off.

ONCE TATER AND I GOT TO THE VAN, I TOOK A MOMENT to try and calm myself down. The caffeine, sugar, and betrayal were a lot to take in all at once. I didn't really have the right to be mad at Mark for moving on or having a job I didn't agree with. We weren't together anymore. I was just embarrassed that my arch nemesis knew more about my ex than I did. And I couldn't help but compare myself to the beautiful Magical woman Bronson was alone in a car with at this exact moment.

We had been alone in a car, thirty minutes ago, and how had that turned out?

After seeing how he lit up talking to her, I knew I couldn't compare to her long legs and sexy vibe. I was complex carbohydrates and gardening. She was lightning and leather.

"Fuck it." I looked back at Tater in the rearview mirror. She wasn't watching the crowd anymore. Instead she focused on me. Her large, soft eyes took me in and saw me for all my pathetic insecurity. I wiped my eyes with the heels of my hands and smoothed my hair, letting the braid out. "Don't tell anyone I have a heart." I laughed. "Hell would freeze over."

With that, I started up the Volkswagen, took a swig of coffee shaking the cubes in the cup, and turned the van around to head to The Row. I needed some time with Beatrice in the pottery studio. I always felt better after working clay with her.

The glow of the coffee had little chance of holding up against the humiliating self-doubt that bloomed inside me.

I shook my head in disbelief at the things I was thinking about myself. *So what if Bronson didn't like me?* I would have preferred that just two days ago. But "Sex Magic" shows up and suddenly, I cared?

I wasn't that girl. I' wasn't the jealous type, but here I was, hightailing it away from the protest to avoid any sighting of Samantha the "Sex Magician."

"Yuck," I said, but Tater wasn't listening. Her attention was on a group of crows that had found perch on a leafless cottonwood tree in the distance. The gray sky defined them in silhouette. It was gloomy... just like my soul.

Why the hell was I even going home? There were two missing person cases and a homicide in my hometown. I had better things to be doing.

I pulled over onto the gravel shoulder. After checking my mirrors, I swung the van wide and aimed it back down the mountain toward Spruce.

I turned the radio on with a satisfying snap. A familiar song with a heavy beat vibrated through the speakers and I tapped my left foot along with the song.

The coffee from The Goose was still ice cold, the cubes jangled with each rut the van hit, and there was half a brownie still tucked into my messenger bag. Things were looking up.

Going downhill, the Vanagon purred. There was less stress on the engine and she cruised along. I was starting to feel hopeful.

But as we rounded the last corner before the straight stretch to Spruce, where we passed the dormant cottonwood, a new sensation of dread spun inside my chest. My feet and hands tingled.

There were more crows now; thirty, forty, a hundred maybe. They covered the branches like aphids. Not a piece of wood was visible under the moving black of beaks and wings.

I slowed the van. My mouth fell open as I looked through the windshield, processing the sight.

Tater had moved to stand between the two front seats. The hair that ran along her spine was standing ridged in a peak of awareness. A low rumble in her chest made the hair on the back of own neck rise.

The poachers I'd saved Tater from had said she couldn't hunt but they'd just had her hunting the wrong thing. She definitely had a nose for magic.

The taste of almonds bloomed in my mouth as the tree, once a convergence of black, erupted into flight removing any indication that a tree had ever been there.

What the hell?

The birds spread the width of the sky and flew northeast.

Chapter Twenty

ANNABETH WATCHED Swell unhitch her mangy dog and make a beeline to Beatrice's Vanagon. She stood in the shop's window, surprised to find herself feeling bad for someone who openly hated her.

Annabeth had always been friends with Mark, but after he got involved with Swell, he'd been distant. She'd always assumed it was because of Swell's influence but in the last two years, she hadn't heard from Mark at all. She'd reached out multiple times, even casually asking his parents when she'd seen them in town. But even they had said, he was very busy and rarely had time to call or visit.

Maybe she'd been wrong. Maybe she had no idea why Mark and Swell had split up. After all, the old saying went, "You never know what goes on behind closed doors."

When Swell had returned to The Row, she kept to herself. The most Annabeth had seen her was once at the grocery store and twice at The Goose, until this last month. Of course, a murder in the Mayback Woods would cause Swell—with her mother's death and job with the Council—to be curious...

Annabeth crossed her arms and watched as Swell wiped her eyes inside the van, flipped a u-ey and headed up the mountain toward home.

Maybe Swell wasn't the cause of her friendship with Mark deteriorating. Maybe Mark wasn't who she thought he was.

Swell wasn't the only person who'd been blindsided by the proposed timber harvest. Mark had placed the offer electronically, never coming home or meeting with her father; no interaction, no emotion.

Annabeth set her plate and cup in the dishbin and exited The Goose.

Maybe it was time to do a little catching up, she thought.

She pulled a cell phone from her pocket and scrolled through the contacts, found Mark's name and sent a text.

THE SLEEK MINI COOPER WASN'T WHAT BRONSON remembered Samantha driving.

"This one?" He pointed to the black car with vanity plates, 'Illumin 8'. "Really, Sam? Isn't that a bit much?"

She waved off his disdain. "It gets great gas mileage and smells like heaven." She slid into the driver's seat. "Plus, I drive so much, I deserve something nice. Bonus points for it being eco-friendly."

"Then get a Prius and nix the vanity plate."

"You've always been a sourpuss." She looked at herself in the rearview mirror, licked her thumb, and wiped under her eyes, removing smudged eyeliner and mascara that had come off in the humidity.

"I didn't expect you to be flashy." Bronson adjusted in his seat. "I took a gamble tipping you off about the sale. If anyone catches on, I could lose my job. And I love my job."

Samantha touched the ignition button, and the little engine roared to life. "You love your job more than the environment?" She shook her head. "Maybe I should be wondering what the hell has happened to you." She said the last word pointedly, but in reality, she was defensive. She knew the car was excessive, but she didn't have any expenses; no home, no children, no pets. She didn't even have more than a week's worth of clothes. She wanted a nice car, and she would defend that with her life.

"I'm not here to fight with you," she said as she steered the small car onto the road that headed toward the park. "We've always been a great team."

Bronson sighed. "I know. I just don't want to mess up a good thing."

Samantha smiled, peeking a look at Bronson as she drove through the outskirts of town. "You mean the girl from The Row?"

Bronson's head snapped up. "She's not a girl."

Samantha laughed. "Oh... so touchy!" She weighed her words carefully. "You like her, don't you?"

But Bronson refused to answer. "I really need to get back to the park. Make sure you drop me off where no one will see. You're as low key as a snake in a pool."

Samantha smiled wider. "You do like her!" She pounded the steering wheel in delight. "I knew it!"

Chapter Twenty-One

THERE WAS a parcel of land that separated the state park from Bronson's land. It was roughly five hectares of prime timber and was owned by Montgomery Lumber Products LLC. The Row Council had been trying to acquire it for over four years and now it was in danger of being logged.

I jogged down the stairs to the R&D office, Tater clipping behind me, to find what looked like a light pole's worth of notes tagged to the board outside my door. My adrenaline evaporated quickly as I shuffled through the notes.

Ilene Frank had called the Council office at least twenty times to inform me that she'd found Markus... with the front of her car. The first message was straightforward but by the fifteenth message, she was full-on snarky.

I started to dial Ilene's number but halfway through the stack, I saw that she was staying at the hospital with Markus Wainwright, since he had no family left in town. Her final note was, "For God's sakes get a cell phone."

There wasn't enough caffeine in the world to sugarcoat a chat with Ms. Frank.

Before I headed to the hospital, I booted up the

computer to check my emails and saw one from Elder Todd's assistant following-up on my report. When the elders had gone to investigate Bronson's property for themselves, they hadn't found anything; not one disturbance, not one redwood.

Which meant that, although Bronson had been there and Beatrice had felt the spell on me when Bronson had brought me home unconscious, it was still my word against theirs. That wouldn't help my reputation. From their perspective it looked like I had overreacted or not been careful enough with a basic ward spell.

I felt the skin on my cheeks flush. I might be an adult, but I felt like I'd always be seen as a child here.

Without a doubt, the ward and the three Elementals had been there. I could get my hackles up and try to prove it (which I really wanted to), or I could go to the hospital and try to get some answers.

With a groan I grabbed my knapsack, slung it over my shoulder, and clipped a leash to Tater's harness. "Let's get some answers," I said. Her bright eyes agreed with my decision.

The Greater Evergreen County Hospital was a rundown monument to the 1960s. Just south of town, the building jutted out of a hillside. It was a bright-white industrial monstrosity that was neither attractive nor practical.

When the lumber industry was in full boom, a hospital was more than necessary. Logging, after all, was a dangerous business.

I don't think the actual design had ever been discussed. When the hospital was built, the town had money to burn and was growing faster than it could handle. I imagined a shitty city architect jumped at the chance to sell the plans, some other town had probably had the good sense to decline.

It looked like a high school that hadn't been painted or renovated since its opening-day ribbon had been cut.

I cracked the windows of the van for Tater and locked the doors behind me.

One long hallway ran north and south, framed by doorways and one long intersecting corridor. The main reception squatted in the middle. I fought the urge to not make eye contact with the receptionist.

I wasn't late for class. I was an adult.

It even smelled like a school, with a hormone-laced anxiety that was almost palpable.

"Can I help you?" an elderly woman wearing a soft pink sweater over a white uniform asked as she smiled. I didn't think she was a nurse; candy striper or volunteer, I bet.

"I'm looking for Markus Wainwright's room?" I could feel my hands subconsciously sliding into my pockets, trying not to touch anything. It was crazy how easily your mind slipped into teen angst.

"Are you family or friend?" Her pink lipstick reflected in the fluorescent light.

"I'm neither. I'm R&D for The Row Council." I shuffled my feet. "Josephine Swell. You can call his room and confirm that I'm welcome."

She regarded me with curiosity. "I'm not familiar with R&D." She cocked her head to the side. "Is it a section of clergy?"

I laughed. "Not exactly. I am a representative of The Row."

"That's lovely dear," she said as she tried to work the ancient computer running on Windows 98.

"Ah, yes. Mr. Wainwright." She tilted her head backward and raised reading glasses to her nose to read from the monitor. "He's in Ward One. I'll just call down." She pivoted in her chair and dialed a large phone that was the color of caramel pudding. The phone didn't ring long before it was answered. She nodded as she spoke, tipping the balance of her curly strawberry-blond hair that was clipped and topped with a cap.

She turned back toward me, her eyes bright with importance. "Mr. Wainwright's room is in Ward One. Room Twenty-eight. Just follow this hall to the end and turn right. The nurse at the station is expecting you." She raised a soft, pink finger to point the direction I was supposed to go.

"Thank you." I rested both of my hands on the knapsack strap and made a mental note to never ever wear that much pink at once, ever in my life. No one should ever look like cotton candy.

"You know, dark colors can make you look older than you are!" she called after me.

"Thanks so much!" I called back. *Touché, lady, touché.*

The nurse at Ward One's nurse's station was dressed in traditional scrubs. Though upon closer inspection, I could see that the polka dots were actually peppermint spirals. I tried not to be creeped out by all the passive-aggressive cheer. Hospitals, after all, were very foreign to people of The Row; magical people in general. We felt we healed faster and better surrounded by the comfort and familiarity of home. But I supposed if you were hit by a Toyota Corolla, like Markus Wainwright, you had no choice in the matter. You went where the ambulance took you.

I could hear Ilene Frank even before I'd reached

Markus's room. She seemed to be watching *Judge Judy* at a high volume and commenting on how she, "...couldn't understand women giving men any money if they didn't even have a job. It was an oxymoron..."

She had a point.

I stood outside the door listening to Ilene relay the show to Markus as he laid on his side, looking out toward the hallway. He was in his early thirties and matched the DMV photo the SPD had forwarded me. He looked like he was in complete agony and it had nothing to do with being hit by a car.

I tapped on the doorframe just before I entered. "Knock-knock!" I tried to sound upbeat and positive to counter the impending onslaught of life advice, I was sure to receive from Judge Judy's biggest fan.

"Glad you could join us," Ilene said, leaning over to open up a bag of Skinny Choice popcorn. "Would it kill you to call a person back? They don't have phones at The Row? You never work?" She waved away my response. "He could have been dead and in the grave by the time you answered your messages. If there was a real emergency, besides what happened with poor Markus here, you'd be the last to know. And what does that say about the Council? That's what I have to say. Quiet now!" She shushed me while she shoveled tiny handfuls of fart-smelling popcorn into her mouth. "Judy's back on."

"Help me!" Markus mouthed silently. He was curled into the fetal position on his side, watching the door like a caged tiger in a zoo.

I smirked. "Hello, Markus. My name is..."

"Josephine," he said, cutting me off. "I know who you are."

"Oh!" I was surprised. "Have we met before?"

"No. But Ilene has been kind enough to tell me all about you during commercial breaks."

He wasn't joking. Not only had she hit him with her car, but she was now slowly killing him with match-making advice and daytime television blasting at full volume.

I raised my finger, begging Markus to hold it together for just a while longer, while I stepped out into the hallway. I returned not more than three minutes later with a wheelchair and a nurse. "Okay, Markus," the nurse said. "It's time to get you up and moving around. We don't want any bedsores."

He looked at me in horror and adoration. Ilene started to roll up her popcorn bag, but I interjected.

"I'll take him for a spin," I said. I looked up toward the television that hung from a metal stand on the concrete wall. "I've seen this episode. You don't want to miss the end." Her eyebrows rose. "The guy who sold the washing machine tries to argue with the judge."

Her head swung back toward the TV to confirm.

"She tells him off," I added hopefully. I could tell I'd distracted her just enough. "We'll be back in fifteen minutes, tops."

I helped the nurse stabilize Markus as he stood on one good leg. The other leg was in a blue soft cast that looked like it weighed as much as a chunk of granite.

Once Markus was securely in the seat and covered with a thin, pastel-peach sheet, I steered him out the door and toward the long corridor. The sound of the television followed us. When we could hear the normal sounds of a hospital and the television was a dim noise in the distance, I could see Markus relax. His head dropped back and his eyes closed.

"I kind of hate and love you," he said.

"There's a club you can join." I grinned and continued wheeling him past the reception area and the pink lady, toward the cafeteria and the outside seating area.

Once the doors closed behind us, Markus took a deep breath. I watched in amazement as he slid his good foot off the footrest and placed it directly onto the ground.

He was grounding. Ironhearts didn't usually use the earth to heal.

"What are you?" I asked.

His eyes weren't thankful anymore. They were angry. "I'm an alchemist. An Earth Alchemist, specifically."

I shook my head. "I don't understand."

"An Earth Alchemist is a cross between an Ironheart and a Magical."

That was news to me.

"They tend to run in a family bloodline." He leaned forward to face me fully. "Magic runs through our blood like a thread. And in the wrong hands, it can be used to magnify magic."

"Bullshit." I shook my head in denial. "There's no such thing."

"Tell that to Abby." His voice was heavy. "She was a good kid, ya know? Smart. Loved the woods and someone killed her." He lowered his voice. "I knew as soon as Abigail was found that what I experienced wasn't just my imagination."

"What happened to you?" I sat down on an ancient metal picnic bench.

"Crows." His voice lowered below a whisper. "I think they can see us. Me... for what I am. I was running from them on my way to The Row's Council office when Lady Tae Bo nailed me with her Corolla."

"You're thirty years old, Markus." I used the heels of my

hands to rub my eyes and took a deep breath. "Why now? Why are the crows just now seeing you?" I made air quotes with my fingers. "It doesn't make sense."

His skin was gray and sickly under the open sky. "I don't know. Both Aldo and Abigail were distantly related to me, and that's too much to be a coincidence. Can we go back inside now?" he asked. "Ilene is safer than those crows, and they'll be looking for me."

It took some finagling, but after one more episode of *Judge Judy* and a total redressing of Markus's bed, I was able to convince Ilene Frank that she should head home and allow Markus some well-deserved silence.

Because he had a hairline fracture, he'd be bedridden for a little while. I suggested Ilene rest up if she was going to bring him home when the hospital released him.

Since her car wasn't drivable, I offered to drive Ilene to impound, where she could get a rental. Her long fingers tapped her gold lamé cigarette case as she considered her next move.

"I can call ahead if you like, to make sure the lot knows you're coming," I said. I could practically hear Markus praying as he held his breath. "If Markus needs anything, he can call you, and you'll be able to come back." Markus's face went pale. "But he's in good hands."

She nodded, making a decision and put the cigarette case and wordfinder paperback into her monogrammed purse. "Sounds good." She pointed a long, sharp nail toward Markus and told him, "If you need anything, you call me."

"I promise," he said, crossing his heart in earnest.

During the day, the impound office served as a rental

car lot and was manned by a young Ironheart by the name of Janice. I'd gone to school with her older sister, and we chatted about what she had been up to while she filled out Ilene's paperwork.

"You don't happen to have Aldo Fuller's truck records, do you?" I asked as she entered info into the database. "It was in impound and then released to family."

Janice's brown eyes closed as she recalled the memory. Then her eyelids snapped open. "I don't need to look those records up. The truck was to be released to next of kin, but with Mr. Montgomery sick and Annabeth taking care of him, Mr. Montgomery called and asked for it to be picked up by a man named Frank Smith."

I leaned forward. "Mr. Montgomery is sick?"

"Oh yes," Ilene Frank butted in. "He is in the advanced stages of Alzheimer's. I'm surprised he was able to call."

How could I have not known he was sick?

"Were you the one who took the call?" I asked Janice.

"Yep," she replied. "I remember it because he'd been concerned about bothering his daughter with it. Mr. Smith came right away and paid to get it released. Easy peasy. No stress for Miss Montgomery."

"Thank you so much Janice." I smiled as nonchalant as I could, knowing in my gut that Mr. Montgomery had never called.

Chapter Twenty-Two

Rain pattered against the roof, waking me up with a muffled drumroll. I folded myself deeper into the covers and listened to the forest outside the house and Beatrice working in her pottery studio below me—the movement of equipment and supplies, the pouring of water, the light clatter of implements collected together, the sliding of the spinning wheel, and finally the rhythmic thumping of Beatrice preparing the clay to be spun.

I slid my legs under the thick comforter and closed my eyes, imagining I was floating in a warm hot spring, weightless, tan, and without a care in the world. No responsibility, no tragedy, no death, no heartache.

My mind jerked away from my daydream to Mark. It was getting harder to remember his face. I could recall the color of his blue polo shirt as it spread across his shoulders, and his long, slender hands with narrow palms that had never felt right in my hands.

A part of me had always known that he wasn't the right person but I'd been scared of losing another person in my life. I'd held on longer than I should have. If anything, living in the city with Mark had confirmed I had no business there, living a half-life away from the land I loved for someone who never tried to understand me.

Maybe I wasn't meant for anyone.

Below, I heard Beatrice slap a lump of clay onto the bat, the scrape of a chair, the splash of water, and finally the click of the wheel engaging as Beatrice's meditative practice began. The mechanics of the wheel whirred me out of my own thoughts and into the plans for the day.

The scrape of nails and an extravagant yawn from the end of the bed, let me know that Tater was also awake and ready for her breakfast.

Maybe if the rain lets up, we could squeeze in a nice walk in the woods...

I raised my hands above me and stretched, surprising myself with a flash of Bronson's profile in my mind. The memory of him at the park, the brush of stiff uniform fabric across the back of my arms. He had felt very warm and very close.

"Okay, Tater!" I said and swung my legs out, over the edge of the bed. "Breakfast!"

Sometimes a bored mind could get a person in trouble.

Tater's ears perked up at the word *breakfast*. She sneezed in agreement and rose to stretch, lowering her nose to the ground and her rump to the sky in a textbook downward dog.

"Show-off," I teased as I stood up stiffly and crossed the room to get ready for the day.

The rain continued through the morning and into midday. It fell in thick, meaty drops, soaking everything it touched. The water filled ditches and streams, that spilled out and over their banks. The roads on the edges of Spruce and the road leading to The Row were mucky and soft, bringing anyone going in and out of The Row to a standstill.

Beatrice, Finn, and I took turns stocking the firebox and tending the woodstove. Beatrice had filled the oil lamps, knowing after years of living here that the small amount of electricity we did have to serve our neighborhood, was easily compromised by falling trees and small landslides.

Beatrice liked to think that it was a necessary time to sit inside, with our thoughts and our feelings. There was a sort of romance to the idea of not being able to carry on with our lives as usual; to be more mindful and contemplative. But after the first day, the romance always faded.

I slipped on a rain suit and stepped into cold rubber boots kept on the front porch. I looked back through the screen door to see Tater watching me. She used her large eyes to guilt me because she knew I wasn't going to take her.

"No way," I said. "I'm not going to be stuck inside with a wet and muddy dog for God knows how many more days. You're staying here."

She huffed once, turned around, and put her rump directly against the door.

"Fine," I said. "Be that way."

I hesitantly crossed the sloppy, wet yard to step onto the gravel ribbon of a lane that meandered through the neighborhood toward the Sanctuary of the Forest Temple. I waved to curious neighbors who watched me from their front windows as I passed.

"Swell!" a woman called from a porch adorned with purple-and-blue painted antler sheds. "Can you please tell Beatrice we'll be doing our group here this month? I don't think I've told her yet."

"No problem!" I called back. Nanette was nice as sugar but mean as a snake if you crossed her. Her husband was an elder on the Council and just as crotchety. I didn't know why they painted the antlers.

Luckily, the path to the sanctuary wasn't flooded out. I jumped over a small stream and entered the gate to the open-air pagoda platform that sat inside a circle of trees and out of view of the road. In the summer, the structure was always pleasant with shade. Two of the sides were walled in to break any wind, rain, or snow from the south. As a child, I would take a book, grab a bundle of blankets from the cupboards along the walls, and cocoon myself into one of the long benches.

The third side was an altar faced north. It was adorned with burning incense, candles that flickered with the energy of spells or prayers, and various small statues of deities people worshiped. The very center point of the floor was painted in the style of tree rings, each ring unique and different. These rings led to a small, darkly stained middle; the heartwood. A perfect place for meditation.

Incense rose slowly to hover just below the roofline, mingling with the rainbow of prayer flags that waved stiffly in the dampness. They were worn and tattered but still quaint. People of the village were good about replacing their own flags with fresh prayers. My white flag, with a bird on it, looked no worse for wear. The bird's silhouette was still crisp against the off-white of the flag. My prayer was still the same.

I slid off my boots and hung my rain gear on the hooks just inside the main entryway. My gardening sweater and wool coat beneath were warm and dry. I grabbed one pillow from the bench on the left and bent to scoop out a warm wool throw from inside the cabinet. I'd brought a hat with me—one that Beatrice had knitted last winter. It was frayed on the edges, but it smelled like home and kept my head warm.

I sat in the middle of the room on the pillow, directly above the heartwood and closed my eyes. I drew in my breath for nine seconds, held it for nine seconds, and then blew it out between pursed lips for nine more seconds. I repeated this nine times. With each cycle of breath, I became more aware of myself and the sounds and movements around me. I kept my eyes closed, hoping to sharpen my instincts. I heard the pattering of rain on the roof after it had filtered down from the tree canopy above. I recognized the thick and lazy drops of rain as they rolled through the gutters and the gurgle of water as it rolled into the waiting ponds and puddles at the base of the downspouts. The trees whistled as wind rushed between them...

The more I focused on what was around me, the warmer I began to feel inside and the more relaxed my body felt.

It was a meditation on cause and effect. A pattern of consequence. The fabric of existence. I wrapped the wool blanket tighter around me, holding in the warmth I had created while focusing my intention. Slowly I opened my eyes, tenderly letting in the gentle light that glimmered through the green hood of the evergreens and waking alders. I felt better now that I'd been able to slosh through the muck and sit without walls enclosed around me. I was free, just like the bird on my prayer flag.

I thought about the feather I'd found on Abigail. That bird hadn't been a symbol of her freedom. Maybe I should check in on her family since their home wasn't very far from the temple.

Markus hadn't been able to hide his connection to

nature...I suspected Abigail had had some secret talents, herself that could help me connect some dots.

Her parents lived at the end of Shannon Lane, which backed up to the edge of the Mayback Woods. A footpath through the woods veered west half a mile from The Row's entrance, directly to their front door.

The path was narrow, bordered by a dense grove of sickly spruce that had been planted by the lumber company. Twenty years later they had grown too close together, choking out the light. What moisture reached the ground left a texture in your nose and mouth—a dry decay you could smell even in summer.

An arch of dead and dying limbs bent above the portal to the trail.

I moved quickly through the opening and down the path, my mind taking liberties with the shadows between the pale trunks. These woods didn't feel healthy. They didn't feel right.

I thought of Abigail walking through these woods, the half-rotten trees guiding her to her death. Had she been alone? Had someone met her?

I moved quickly toward the end of the path into a clearing, where the Steele's home sat. The light from the sky barely penetrated to the center of the lawn. I stopped short, pausing at the stillness of the house. No lights burned in the windows. No smoke rose from the chimney, and there was no car in the drive. Rainwater had accumulated at the base of the home. None of the ground or drive looked disturbed. I didn't think anyone had been home for days.

Wouldn't the Council have been told if the Steeles were

leaving town? People in Spruce were nosy. Surely someone would have noticed. Wouldn't they?

Just to be sure, I waded through the wet grass to the porch and waited, listening for sound inside. I heard no movement, but the feeling of being watched permeated the clearing. I looked around toward the back of the house, but nothing moved.

I stepped up onto the porch, trying with all my might to appear calm, and knocked on the front door. Nothing moved inside.

The fencing around the yard looked secure, but the goats and chickens were quiet. I crossed the porch, stepped off the rail-less deck, and followed the side of the house to the backyard. I stopped at the gate to look into the goat and chicken pens. They were empty.

Unease pulled across my chest once again.

"Mr. Steele?" I called. "Rebecca?" My voice passed my lips and stuck in the thick stillness.

The dark clouds that had been offshore were approaching. The house and the area around it was drawn in shadow. "Hello?"

I looked across the backyard and the pens again to focus on the back porch and windows. Abigail's window was drawn tight.

My intuition screamed at the heaviness. It was as if I'd just missed a thunderclap and the static still charged the air around me. I fought the urge to run as I realized just how secluded I was behind the wall of trees.

I shouldn't be here.

I searched the tree line that bordered the property. There was no one here. No one except me and the darkness that watched from the edges and seemed to move between the sickly trunks.

I was alone and without my hiking stick. I didn't dare pull energy to ward myself from within the semicircle. No doubt it was tainted from whatever wrapped around the house and nearby woods.

But below my raincoat I wore my coat with the charged copper clasps. They would be the only energy source I could use that wouldn't be directly influenced by my surroundings. Gently I released the snap of the rain jacket and swiped my fingers across the first clasp. I felt its energy absorb into me with ease. I ran my fingers past the second and third clasps, powering up. The warmth of their energy was a comfort that pushed away the chill in my fingers and toes.

I looked toward the front of the house one more time, hoping to pull off a pensive, but not alarmed, expression. With the house behind me and the dark path before me, the feeling of being watched was overwhelming. I wanted to speed through, afraid that hands would reach out between the trees and grab me. Halfway through the tunnel, I began to see spots and realized I'd forgotten to breathe. I knew that the tunnel wasn't the end of my journey home but just the first steps toward safety. I could only pray I'd be fast enough.

Ten feet from the entrance to the lane, movement to my right caught me by surprise. I stumbled and skidded in the thick muck between the spindly roots. A flutter of wings. A blur of black.

I glanced back to see three black birds perched on stunted limbs. They watched with flat, beady eyes and sharp beaks, not making a sound.

The air on the outside of the property line was immediately lighter, brighter, and cleaner. I thought for a split second that maybe I had been overreacting, but the birds hopped down, soundlessly moving between branches, unsettling decay that rained down like fine powder. One crow, the smallest, hopped between the bases of the trees to observe me more closely. The small lenses of its eyes blinked, each time focusing directly onto my face. It ruffled its feathers, bobbing up and down, as it bounced to rest in the middle of the path. The other two flittered between perches, nearly eye level to me. Their claws strangled the limbs, leaving indentations in the bark as they moved to keep up with me.

The larger bird spread its wings and took off, swooping past me and causing me to duck.

"Go! Shoo!" I shouted.

But they only seemed to become more persistent, dive-bombing me as I walked down the lane, farther away from the Steeles' homestead.

I pulled a little more energy from the copper clasps and raised an imaginary boundary out of my body. I could see it in my mind's eye like a thin membrane or bubble that pushed out, impenetrable, to stabilize my immediate area.

I wasn't going to run from three mean crows on my own turf. I put my bare hands together, rubbing them counter-clockwise until the heat throbbed between my palms. With my feet I drew an X in the mud and sunk my feet deep into the muck, grounding myself, and clapped my hands. The heat in my hands was almost unbearable.

The satisfying weight of the mud was cool and calming on my feet through the boots. The spell would, in theory, scramble the crows' ability to sense where I was, distorting my body heat. A balance of hot and cold, earth and sky, was a spell to confound the eye.

The birds turned in midair, unsure of where they needed to be. They could sense me but weren't able to pinpoint my exact location. Glossy blue-black wings reflected the bright, jarring light that cut through a break in the clouds. They spun around each other, communicating their confusion.

They silently cawed to each other, spiraling in the air until they cut sharp ninety-degree turns, returning to their master like dark vapors against the billowing charcoal-gray sky.

Chapter Twenty-Three

"Your job ISN'T to solve the death of an Ironheart. You aren't the finder of old men who made a living cutting down trees! You aren't their champion!" Elder Todd's skin pulled against his geriatric blue veins as he yelled. "Your JOB is to make sure no one on The Row is hel... er... is practicing blood magic!"

His voice stumbled but his rage stayed the same as he continued to yell at me. "Leave the affairs of Ironhearts to the SPD and stay the course. Your job is to ensure that peace remains between Spruce and The Row during a time when we are perilously close to losing this land sale! And now protestors?"

He slammed his hand down onto the desk. Large golden rings dwarfed his fingers. He looked frail, but I knew that he wasn't. His ability to summon the elements was well-known. Well-known enough to keep him comfortable in a position that he'd grown complacent in.

"YOUR job," he continued, "is to sniff out illegal magic and clean it up, not to stick your nose where it doesn't belong. If those trees end up cut, it is because of your actions today!"

"Today?" I spoke for the first time.

Elder Todd, looked up at me as if he'd forgotten I was there. "Crows are just crows, Josephine. Stop embarrassing yourself."

A knock at the door pulled Hot Toddy's attention from me.

"Your appointment is here," Diedre, Elder Todd's assistant, said.

I didn't know how long she'd been standing in the doorway.

"We're finished here." Elder Todd waved me away with the back of his hand.

I felt the flush of my cheeks. I'd promised myself no one would talk to me like that again. "I'm sorry, I didn't quite catch that," I said, trying not to let my voice crack. "Did you just say I was doing a great job? Aww thanks! Don't mention it."

"You'd be wise to change your tone." Elder Todd's voice was sharp against my pride.

"I'll change my tone when you change yours. Respect is earned, Señor Todd."

My fucking mouth always got me in trouble. But this was good trouble. I turned to look Diedre, his evil lackey, in the eye for good measure but blanched at the sight of Annabeth Montgomery waiting next to her.

As per usual, Annabeth was sunshine and polish, and I felt as fresh as dog shit.

"What are you looking at?" I said rolling my eyes as I pushed past her.

My heels dug into the wood floor as I stormed toward my office. *Why the hell did we have wood floors if we were trying to stop the practice of clear-cutting?* The hypocrisy of it made me sick.

Not sick enough to stop me from scarfing down two wedges of Toblerone and the remains of a lukewarm coffee from The Goose, I had back in my office. I wanted my dog. Tater would have had my back. She wouldn't have let Montgomery sneak up behind me.

I wanted to hide in my office. I wondered if I could go out the window. I hated how I felt when Elder Todd talked to me like that. I hated how I felt when I reacted the way I had. It wasn't healthy to allow people to abuse you, no matter what their position was. They could be my boss or my subordinate, but they should be safe around me and vice versa.

I'd also been a jerk to Annabeth. Granted, she was evil... but that didn't give me the right to talk to her like I had. Now that I knew about her father, I realized I'd been too hard on her.

Chapter Twenty-Four

ANNABETH's earliest memories began below a cherry tree that grew stubbornly outside her father's front door. Her father had spent his entire adult life cutting down trees, but this tree grew steadily skyward, twisting up and around the old home's eaves.

As an adult, she had built a small swinging bench below it and sought the safety of that spot to clear her mind.

Her father's diagnosis had changed everything for them. She'd been halfway through her senior year in college when a call had brought Annabeth home, putting school on hold in the city. Instead of a teacher, Annabeth had become her father's primary caregiver.

Richard Montgomery had raised Annabeth with a cold remoteness one would see in a benefactor, after her mother had died. It would have killed her father to be this vulnerable in front of his daughter—if he could still remember that he had a daughter.

Annabeth leaned back, resting her bare feet on the ground and her head on the swing's smooth wooden headrest. Nothing in her world made sense anymore, but swinging back and forth, looking up at the limbs above her, gave her a sense of stability. The tree continued to flourish, and it felt like home.

She closed her eyes and listened to the sound of life around her; the neighbors mowing lawns, children playing, the breeze gently moving through the tree above her, the wind chime that hung on the front stoop.

Life was going on around her, but her world wasn't. Her life had stopped the day she'd come home. Maybe that was why she'd taken out her frustration on Swell today.

When she'd heard that Swell had broken things off with Mark and come home to The Row, she'd been furious. Who would willingly give up life in the city with a good guy? Not her.

What better way to avoid the bad in her own life than to direct it toward someone else? That's what she'd been doing but it didn't feel right anymore.

She had kept her father's illness a secret for a long time, making excuses and fabricating stories of trips and meetings he was in, to people who asked. When her car broke down near the viewpoint in the snow this past winter, there had been no one to call. For the first time she'd felt wholly alone, and it scared her.

When Finnigan Swell had pulled up in his ratty Volkswagen truck, fiddled under the hood of her car, and offered to tow her back to town, she'd been grateful.

But she'd also been smitten. The inside of Finnigan's truck had smelled like freshly turned soil, and he spoke to her in a way that had made her feel safe. He'd reminded her of the cherry tree she'd contemplated under her entire life.

Now dozing under the same tree, she thought about how she'd burned quite a few bridges between Finn's sister and herself. Why would Josephine ever accept her? Would

Finn have been so kind to her if he had known how horrible she'd been to Swell?

It was a fine mess. One that Annabeth wanted to fix. She wanted to see Finn again, and she hoped he felt the same way.

Annabeth gathered a sweater and her father's truck keys from inside. She stopped to kiss her sleeping father on the forehead and checked in with the nurse before she left. Weekly respite care gave her time to run errands and grab a coffee. It also gave her an excuse to shower.

The eyes that looked back at her in the rearview mirror looked confident and sure to some, but they looked haunted to her. She'd never expected to be a caregiver in her twenties, instead of in graduate school. She was thankful to be able to care for him and loved him dearly, but the intensity of the responsibility weighed heavily on her. It was devastating to helplessly watch a once vibrant man, who'd single-handedly started and grown a formidable logging company, silently slip away.

The truck idled high, forming a large cloud of exhaust in the rearview. She needed to go to the bank, the post office, and the pharmacy. If the weather allowed, she could drive to a bigger city, forty-five minutes to the north, to pick up home health care supplies.

Waiting at the only stoplight in town, her fingers thrummed along the steering wheel to the beat of a song on the radio. Cross traffic slowed and the light changed to green. Annabeth eased the beast of a vehicle through the intersection, noticing a blue and white Ford F150 waiting to turn northeast toward the state park. The back end was full of large industrial-grade chainsaws. She recognized the shapes out of habit and wondered where they were headed. Would they be cutting the parcel of land her father had sold to Mark?

She realized with a start that Mark never responded to her text. They hadn't been best of friends, but they'd been close. It wasn't like the Mark she'd known her whole life, to ghost her.

It wasn't her business though, was it? She squeezed the steering wheel and sighed. She wanted to turn around and see where the truck was headed, but forced herself to keep the wheel straight, toward the post office. She told herself to focus on the tasks at hand and let the professionals do their jobs, even if those "professionals" happened to include the sister of the guy she couldn't stop thinking about. The sister who hated her freaking guts.

Chapter Twenty-Five

Rays of twilight drifted through a marine haze, illuminating the trunks of trees and sides of houses. The golden hour promised longer days and shorter nights, but the sun had passed behind the horizon almost an hour ago and Finn wasn't yet home. Beatrice had finished making a thick red chili hours before, the house smelling of spice and heat as she portioned out the cooled stew into containers and placed them into the fridge. It wasn't like Finn to miss dinner. His internal clock worked around food, so when he'd failed to come home in time for dinner, I started to worry.

One by one, the windows of neighboring houses began to warmly glow as lights were turned on or lamps lit. I watched restlessly for Finn's truck lights as I thumbed through the heritage reports of family trees under the flame of an oil lamp. I traced the names from top to bottom and bottom to top with my fingers. The lines between Ironhearts and Magicals intersected occasionally, but they were easy to follow. It was shocking how segregated we remained.

The light in the kitchen went out and the familiar

sounds of Beatrice moving through the house comforted me, even as an adult. Beatrice frowned as she paused next to me.

"I'm going to bed, dearest. You shouldn't be wasting your time worrying about your brother like an anxious parent." Her hair was pulled into an elegant braid, the plaits pinned into a soft chignon at the base of her neck. "He can take care of himself. You should be worried about yourself... and that love life you've failed to tend."

I snorted. "What love life?"

"That man friend who's nice to look at. Smells good too."

I blushed, suddenly feeling defensive. "Beatrice!"

"If you can't talk about how he looks or smells ... you probably shouldn't be looking at his backside so hard in public."

"I did not!" I exclaimed. But I'd caught myself looking, so I wasn't shocked that she had seen it too.

"You're a terrible liar, Swell." Beatrice watched me. "I hope you can let yourself love someone again. I don't worry about Finn, but you ... You're becoming a rock in a river. Stubborn and unmoving."

"I'm fine, thanks."

"Well, the rock gets worn down eventually. Maybe the ranger will be persistent enough to rub you down."

"Oh my God!" I wanted to disappear.

She smiled and patted me on the shoulder. "Don't be an island, sweetheart. You need to love someone as much as you need to be loved. Now, go to bed and leave that brother of yours safe from the inquisition tonight."

The more Beatrice ran defense for Finn, the more I realized she knew exactly where he was. But I did want to go to bed. Tater had gone up an hour before, and I knew from experience that if I nudged her over, I could steal the warm spot on the bed under the covers.

"Maybe a reprieve until the morning." I piled the papers up and placed a chunk of raw rainforest jasper on top, just in case there was a draft in the night.

I tucked my feet into soft fleece slippers and bent to blow out the oil lamp that extinguished with a tender pop. I followed Beatrice, her lamp warming the space around her as she rounded the corner. I found my way to the stairs and climbed them by the soft light of a waning moon.

By the time I woke up and got down to the kitchen the next morning, Finn's telltale cereal bowl and signature cup were in the sink.

"Did I miss him?" I asked, looking out the front window to the driveway.

"Who, dear?" Beatrice was being evasive.

"You know who. The only other person who lives here with us." I probably sounded more cross than I should have.

"Oh, Finn. Yes, he's gone for the day. He said he was heading to the city for some seed stock and garden supplies." She was dressed for yoga and was making Tater sit and stay for pieces of Tofurky.

"You shouldn't feed her that."

"She likes it." Beatrice tossed a piece of withered tofu bacon into Tater's waiting mouth.

"It's not good for her." I rummaged around for the coffee press, but it wasn't where I'd left it in the cabinet. "Have you seen my French press?" I asked over my shoulder.

"It's in the cabinet."

"It's not there." I opened each cupboard, drawer, and even the fridge. The coffee press was gone.

Either the house fae had declared war on me or someone was trying to make me emotionally unstable.

"You know, Finn said that house fae had taken my chocolate and coffee beans the other day. But now the press too?" I stabbed a box of English breakfast tea with a butter knife.

"House fae aren't after you," Beatrice said, breaking one final piece of Tofurky into two pieces and signaled Tater to lay down for reward. The dang dog laid down and rolled onto her back, legs in the air.

"Overachiever," I grumbled.

"What was that, dear?" Beatrice asked.

"Nothing. Just questioning all my life choices."

I put the kettle on to boil and waited for the subpar caffeine substitute to be ready. I couldn't even consider using any more energy to take a shower.

"There are raspberry scones in the basket if you're hungry," Beatrice offered.

But even pastries couldn't warm my frigid heart this morning without coffee.

The sound of tires on gravel pulled my attention to the front yard. I couldn't see a car but a door slamming confirmed that someone was here. I shuffled barefoot to the front door and swung it open, expecting to see Finn. But I stumbled back to hide behind the door when Bronson, with a coffee in each hand, rounded the corner of the porch.

"Morning, Swell... I come bearing gifts and glad tidings!" He lightly shook the iced coffee, and I realized how similar I was to Tater, being manipulated into tricks for treats. I wouldn't be as indiscreet as Tater, however.

"What do you want?" I peered around the edge of the

heavy black door, trying to minimize how much of my ruddy, unwashed face showed.

"Just came for a visit." He smiled, and I ignored the warmth on the top of my head.

"I'm not showered."

"I can wait." He extended the arm with the iced coffee, his smile wider.

I regarded him for a moment and then looked down at myself in jammies with bare feet. "Whatever." I snatched the coffee and walked back to the kitchen to turn off the kettle, and grabbed a scone as I went upstairs to shower. "I'll be ready in twenty minutes. Scones are in the basket. Don't give any to Tater. She's already eaten too much junk this morning."

I could hear him chuckle as Beatrice and Tater greeted him. The sound of Tater jumping and whining with delight made me happy. Happier than I had been with just tea.

I DRESSED IN LAYERS AND TIED MY STILL-WET HAIR into a bun that dripped down the back of my neck. It left a ring of damp around the collar of a clean sweatshirt that sported a unicorn cage-fighting a phoenix. It was from a band I'd seen in concert when I'd lived in the city, and I couldn't decide if I related more to the magical horse with a rainbow horn or the poster child for repeated rock-bottom burnouts. The band's name had been "Caged Magic" but they'd really been canned crap. I'd bought a CD too and played it when I was feeling emo.

"Cool sweatshirt," Bronson said as I came down the stairs.

I didn't say anything. I pulled deeply on the last draught

of the coffee and tossed the remaining ice into the sink, careful to leave the plastic cup in the recycle/upcycle bin Beatrice used for art projects.

"How'd you know that I needed coffee?" I asked, catching him only slightly off guard.

"Finn gave me a heads-up that you'd pissed off a domestic portion of the Good Neighbors and that coffee would be the best way to get on your good side."

"Wanna go for a drive?" I asked.

"What do you have in mind?"

"I have a case I'm working on, and I need to check in on a witness."

"That sounds intriguing... Are you asking for the company or the ride?"

I smiled wider, a giggle rumbling in my chest. "A little of both." I grabbed the messenger bag, the stack of heritage records, and Tater's leash. I didn't even need to call her. She was already ahead of me, heading out the door toward Bronson's truck.

"Shouldn't you leave Tater here?"

"No dog, no deal." I pulled sunglasses from the inside of my bag and perched them on my nose, smugly smiling when the door shut behind me and Bronson followed without further complaint to the truck and the impending eighty-pound storm of dog hair that waited for him.

For a moment, I thought Ilene Frank might pass out. She'd opened the door expecting me but instead found all six feet of smoldering park ranger staring back at her in the doorway.

"Mrs. Frank," I said.

"Miss," she corrected me.

I cleared my throat and continued. "This is Ranger Wise. He's assisting me with Markus's... umm... issue."

"Pleasure, pleasure," she said. Each word was drawn out in a purr. She smiled widely and glided backward to open the door. "Please," she said, "come in, won't you?" She never took her eyes off of Bronson, who was confused and looking a little scared.

I giggled.

"How's the patient doing?" I asked.

"Eating me out of house and home."

"Well, you did almost kill me," Markus said from the couch. "It's the least you could do."

Ilene glared at Markus and then looked back at Bronson to explain. "I love to cook. It's always a treat to make a meal for a hungry man." She touched his forearm and batted her eyelashes.

Bronson stilled, and I thought I saw color drain from his face but he recovered well, patting her hand. "That's very kind of you," he said. "Markus is very lucky to have you in his life."

I heard a snort from the couch. "Lucky my ass."

"How are you feeling?" I asked. He looked miserable.

"Not dead and not being pecked to death by crows, so things are looking up."

"You look much better today," I lied.

"You're a terrible liar," Markus said.

I liked this guy.

"Have you had a chance to go outside today?"

"No," Markus said. "Nurse Ratched won't let me do anything by the windows. She's worried her yard gnomes could get crapped on by the birds." He pulled himself up on the couch. "Her priorities are seriously skewed."

"Well, you did destroy her car," I said.

While Ilene was distracted asking Bronson if he wanted coffee or a bowl of Jell-O salad, I slipped a sunstone into Markus's hand. "Its energy should help," I said. "I'll bring another when I can."

Chapter Twenty-Six

After Bronson dropped me off, the house felt very quiet. I decided to take Tater with me for a run to get my mind right.

The path to the top of the mountain was fairly even, and even though there were drop-offs, it would still be a good place to run her and get some of her energy out. She patiently waited for the harness, but when I brought out the leash, her back end nearly touched her nose with the force of her wagging as I clipped it on.

I put on light rain gear since the weather was a tad wetter and drearier than it had been the day before, and stretched on the front porch. I tugged my hat down onto my head and flipped up the rain hood. I tapped the tip of Tater's nose with my finger and asked, "Ready, girl?"

Her eyes were pools of mischief reflecting back at me. I leaned down and gave her a kiss on the head. "Let's go!" And with that, her large paws sunk into a thin layer of mud and loose gravel, and we darted through the garden and into the fray. We startled the ducks that pitched and quacked.

They rose slightly off the ground, gliding heavily to the ground ten feet from where we sped.

"Sorry!" I called back.

I wouldn't need music today. The forest was dancing. The moisture weighed down the limbs, which tipped until the balance of the added weight slid the water in a stream down off the branches. It cascaded to limbs that bounced down below. The rhythm sped us on.

Tater was doing well, navigating the roots and trees without tangling herself up in the brush. When we reached the deepest part of the forest, near where the solstice celebration would be held, we stopped to take a break and watch the trees around us expand and breathe. The woods around us were alive with celebration, their cells expanding with light and water, applauded by the sound of rain cascading to the ground below.

It was hard to leave. Once we'd stood still long enough, tiny birds, squirrels, and other small mammals began to move about in the area around us. Tater stayed by my side, but her head and ears followed the sounds and sights.

I stretched again to keep from cramping up later. Tater took my lead and rose up her back legs to stretch her front. She did a huge yawn that exposed her back teeth and shook herself. "Oh! What a big stretch!" I cheered. Her tail swayed side to side in thanks. Then we reluctantly moved on.

Down the path we jogged, passing huge root balls and nurse logs with gaping holes that disappeared into the ground. We hopped over smaller downed trees and under tangles of larger ones. The closer we got to the boundary of the woods, the more light filtered through spires of sickly trees left behind as subpar or stream buffers. The trees that hadn't fallen in the first windstorms, after their neighbors had been clear-cut jutted up in awkward angles, weighed down by conks and other fungi.

The quarter-mile sprint to the very top from this side of the ridge was brutal, and I second-guessed my choice. I leaned onto the balls of my feet, using my arms to counterbalance the momentum as I trudged joyfully up.

"Ah! Tater! We made it!" I wheezed. But she didn't seem to share my pride. She was thirsty.

I hadn't thought to bring water.

Luckily, the spring was close by. I guided Tater across the clearing to the outcropping and followed the same path I'd used before.

The jangle of Tater's halter seemed extraordinarily loud in the stillness of the amphitheater of trees that surrounded the small spring, which bubbled softly. The hair on the back of my neck rose with the awareness that we were not welcome.

I paused, watching for any movement. The space seemed to be waiting. At my feet, Tater released a deep rumble; the growl pulling at the magic in me.

I spread my awareness outward, searching for the pull of anyone or anything near, but I wasn't able to focus my intention. There was a disruption of energy around us. Tater growled deeper and louder this time. Her focus was on the spring.

I'd had enough. "Show yourself!" I shouted to break the weight of stillness, knowing I'd feel silly if it was just a deer or bunny. But nothing moved and no one stepped into the amphitheater. Dim light through the trees laid shadows like lace on the ground.

"Last chance." I wasn't shouting anymore. I knew whoever it was, was close.

The shadows on the ground distorted for just a moment

—enough time for me to get a bead on where the hidden person was. I took my chance. My fingers curled around the moonstone in my pocket, as I whispered an incantation, "Above, below, and far between, remove the spell to see the unseen."

The disconcerting pressure of a glamour meeting resistance slipped past my skin like a tight wetsuit to reveal a wide-eyed, emaciated ghost of a man who gasped in desperation as he realized he was no longer hidden.

Aldo Fuller dropped to his knees and sobbed. In horror, I realized he hadn't been missing. He had been hidden against his will.

"Can you see me?" he asked between sobs. "Can you see me?" I could hear raw panic in his voice.

Tater's leash pulled from my hand as she ran across the clearing to put her face deeply into Aldo's chest. She licked and prodded him with her nose, whined and whimpered. I took off my jacket and wrapped it around the man's thin, fragile frame. Large wrinkled hands covered his face, leaving only the long gray beard peeking below. Tater's enthusiasm knocked him off balance, and his hands dropped to steady himself. His fingers wove into her coat as deep, wracking sobs shook his entire body.

"I see you. You're safe," I said, trying to sound calm.

The magic that had been used to cast this spell had a source of infinite power that ran off of Aldo himself. His energy had been a battery that wouldn't run out of juice until the spell was broken or Aldo himself had expired. It was a very complex spell that needed energy that continually affected the area around it.

"Do you think you can make it to The Row?" I asked.

He nodded. His cornflower-blue eyes met mine. "I think I could fly."

Aldo was able to walk to Beatrice's with minimal help. He looked frail, but he was still strong. Agile even. He'd gone over and under logs easier than I had, and with each step Tater was just in front of him, guiding the way.

Close to the trailhead, we both stopped to observe a group of crows circling in the air not too far from where we'd been, interested in something below.

"They aren't normal crows, those," Aldo said. He turned away, maneuvering over a large root to follow Tater. "They're looking for me." His long fingers were curled around a stick of alder that he used as a makeshift cane. "They dogged me for days after I'd gone, gone." He wiped his mouth with the back of his hand. "They couldn't see me, but they knew I was there. They could smell me."

Beatrice was waiting for us at the back door. In her arms was a thick wool blanket that she'd warmed next to the fire. She wrapped it around Aldo in greeting. "I've been so cold" he said. Beatrice guided him to a large cushioned chair next to the fireplace, where he sat, leaning toward the fire. "Don't get too close, now," she warned softly. "I don't want you getting dehydrated." She placed a small bowl of soup into his hands. The long bony fingers curled around the pottery. He was weak, but his hands didn't shake holding the bowl. With one hand, he raised the spoon to his mouth.

"Porcini," he whispered. He looked up to make eye contact with Beatrice. "You made me mushroom soup."

"Welcome home, Aldo," she said and smiled, placing warm bread on the end table next to him. "Eat slow, friend."

I sat back, watching Aldo as Tater circled to lay at his feet. Beatrice continued to stoke the fire, humming as she moved around the room. How could a man have been missing for so long, unable to communicate, made it this long? It was possible he'd been able to endure, pulling from his experience in the woods. But to survive the unforgiving elements of nature while being hidden with a parasitic spell... It was truly remarkable.

I wanted to ask him so many questions... I didn't want to take my eyes off him, for fear he would disappear again.

Once he nodded off, Beatrice came to sit beside me in the kitchen. "What a lucky man," she said as she portioned two small bowls of soup—one for each of us from the pot on the stove. Her brow was pinched with worry.

"What aren't you saying?" I asked. The ladle paused midway between the pot on the stove and the bowl.

She sighed heavily. "I don't think our friend was targeted with that spell." She looked back over her shoulder at Aldo, her eyes sad. "I think it's possible he might have done it to himself."

I started to argue.

"He didn't mean to do it, I'm sure," She wiped her hands on a well-worn apron. "But a spell like that isn't thrown around without a great amount of power. That spell reeks of fear, and fear is powerful."

She placed a bowl in front of me, slipping a spoon into the cream. "It reminds me of the ward you tripped," she said.

"Could an Ironheart be able to set a ward like that?" I asked as I sat up straighter.

Beatrice thought for a moment, taking a spoonful of soup. "Not intentionally, no."

"Have you ever heard of something called Earth Alchemy?" I watched her reaction to the term pass across her face.

"There have always been rumors, but they have been just that."

We sat in silence, finishing our soup and sneaking

glances at the thin man that slept deeply in front of the fire place.

I picked up our empty bowls and set them in the sink. Beatrice leaned into her chair and rocked back and forth. The sounds of the house and the crackle of the fire were deceptively comforting.

"There's a guy in town who says it isn't a rumor," I said.

"Then you better make sure the ingredients aren't easily obtained."

I nodded. *Ingredient* was a sterilized term, but it was exactly how the caster would think of Aldo and Markus.

With the solstice celebration and the full moon occurring soon, I had to make sure both Aldo and Markus were in a safe place until I figured out what exactly was going on. Magic was more potent with the cycles of the moon and the seasons. It was more likely this new "big bad" would be looking to take advantage of the boost in their spells. Anyone with a hint of Earth Alchemy in their bloodline wouldn't be safe.

I called Ilene Frank from the house phone and asked if she'd be up for an additional houseguest. After she gave me a lesson in manners and hospitality expectations, she agreed. I could hear Markus in the background asking to talk to me, but Ilene either had grown hard of hearing or was enjoying the power play. Either way, I knew Markus was safer with that chain-smoking bulldog, than alone at his house. Aldo could recuperate near friends and it didn't hurt that Ilene wouldn't let anyone in or out without first exhausting them with guilt. It was a good security system.

Chapter Twenty-Seven

I WOKE up feeling the pull of the solstice celebration. There was a heat in the air as the marine layer burned up under the sunlight. The energy of a full moon and the summer solstice lining up at the same time was distracting. Beatrice had always said it was nature's pheromones, and I couldn't help but agree. It felt like a courtship.

I opened up the cedar chest and lifted out my ceremonial white dress, which was basically a potato-sack shape with straps instead of sleeves. It fell about mid-calf. Though, it was preferred that members of The Row were unclad for ritual, a ceremonial dress was just as acceptable. The dress was soft and smelled of jasmine, sandalwood, and the woods.

My ritual cloak was a deep forest green. It had been hand-sewn by Beatrice's grandmother and handed down to me. I was convinced that there was a little extra mojo in it after all the celebrations it had been in. Every time I put it on, I felt a snap of energy, like static. I stood in the mirror and slipped the cloak on, annoyed with myself for wondering if Bronson would be there. I judged my face and skin and was disappointed to see my face with freckles. A tendril of anxiety spiked within me, and I shook my head to press it down.

I looked myself in the eye and said, "You and your freckles are just fine." I then rolled my eyes and placed the cloak and dress on hangers and hung them up to let the wrinkles relax out.

I smoothed my t-shirt and khaki shorts, slipped into my favorite pair of Birkenstocks, and grabbed my iron dagger, clipping it to my belt. I pulled on my gardening sweater and rumbled down the stairs above the pottery studio, down into the kitchen.

"Beatrice!" I called out, "I'm going to fetch flowers and feathers!"

I heard movement in the hallway just past the studio, which was Beatrice's room.

"I'm coming too!" I heard her call as a galloping dog came bounding down the hallway toward me, tongue lolling out and tail wagging. She'd gained a good ten pounds since I'd gotten her out of impound. Her golden coat was now shiny and had hints of red in the light.

"You are such a pretty girl," I said as I crouched low to the ground in front of her and smushed her cheeks toward her nose. It wrinkled up into an adorable smoochy face, and I kissed her dry nose. She sneezed, shaking her head and licking her nose, which was now covered in slobber.

"Don't tell anyone that I said that." She tilted her head in question, and I smiled. "Us pretty girls need to stick together." She barked, tilting her butt up in the air and her front end low to the ground, stretching. Then she turned and ran full speed through the kitchen and out toward the garden.

"Beatrice!" I called out. "We'll be in the garden!"

"All right, dear!"

The back door was already open, and Tater was playfully chasing the drakes around the squash bed. They quacked and flapped their wings while she bounced after them like a bunny, barking each time she rose.

Beatrice had already gathered the baskets, which sat on the back porch. They were large-mouthed made of woven materials and dyed in various bright colors. The handles were leather, and they smelled of summer.

I scooped up the large pink-and-turquoise one, my favorite. I hoped to find some St.-Johns-wort, the herb of sunshine, though it was probably too early yet in the season. But it had been warmer earlier, so I was hopeful. I moved between the garden beds, the ducks, stray flower pots, and an ever-moving Tater toward the tree line in the back of the yard. It was the boundary of the woods, but also where a nice assortment of berries and wild herbs grew.

I could see thimbleberry leaves, large and bright green, yarrow (an umbrella of small, happy, white parasol flowers), and bright new growth on cedar leaves. I wanted to wait for Beatrice to begin but hummed the harvest song as I took the time to look at the base of the trees for anything that could be used. I gathered a few supple cedar bows, as well as some moss that had been displaced during the last winds.

As I foraged, I thought about Markus and Aldo. I'd called twice since I'd delivered Aldo to his "bodyguard," but each time, Ilene had assured me "her men" were just fine.

"No one in or out. Even if you know them," I reminded her the second time I'd called.

"Do I look like an idiot? I have nightgowns older than you" she snapped back.

"Okay..." It took me a second to shake the image. "I'll be

at the ceremony, but if you need anything, you can call Officer Trigger. He's on duty tonight."

"Yeah, yeah. I got the number."

Eventually, Beatrice joined me in the garden, bringing with her damp and pliant hemlock roots, dried herbs, and an iced coffee for both her and me. After we filled our baskets with flowers, leaves, and feathers, we sat on the back porch watching the landscape change. The warmth of the sun ebbed away, and the clicking of insects and the chirp of birds replaced the sounds of the day. We took spruce roots that Beatrice had soaked in water—blessed by the sun and moon—and wrapped them, weaving and braiding them to create the bare bones of our solstice crowns.

I tried not to linger or think about Aldo and how thin he'd been or the crows that had crossed the expanse between the spruce trees just south of the garden.

I watched Beatrice's hands, artful and deft, easily manipulate the pliant cords. Her mother had been taught by elders of this land's first people, how to harvest the roots and how to prepare them. It was a skill we continued to pass down, with respect.

Every time I was amazed at how seamlessly Beatrice could create something so beautiful. Even now, as an adult, I still asked for help and guidance. But this year, my mind wandered to darker places. To the day when Beatrice wouldn't be there to calmly and lovingly guide me, as I wove the crowns together like a dance.

The thought of doing this alone created an empty ache inside my breast. How could I possibly continue existing without her one day?

When the doorbell rang, I was shocked to see Annabeth Montgomery at our door. Finn barreled down the staircase from his room, getting to her first. I noticed he'd showered and put on his dress clothes. His feet, however, were still bare.

Startled, I stepped back. "Doing house calls now?" I asked her, still not catching on to what was happening.

Annabeth, dressed in a soft yellow dress that hung to mid-calf, blinked, breaking eye contact with Finn. Her eyes met mine for only a moment before fluttering down to look at her own bare feet.

What the fresh hell?

"Please come in," Finn said. His movements were awkward and stiff. "We are just about to head up to the clearing."

"Oh good," she said with a heavy sigh. I realized she'd been holding her breath. "I was worried I was going to be late."

Finn led her through our small parlor and into the kitchen. I trailed behind, mouth open, realization oozing over me.

"I would have waited for you," Finn said. I only caught tidbits of what they were saying. There was a giggle.

Oh, hell no.

Now I knew why Beatrice had made extra solstice crowns. "For friends," she'd said. I didn't want to wrap my mind around it.

"Oh, Annabeth! So wonderful to have you join us!" Beatrice hugged her, pulling the twig of a girl into an embrace that would have snapped a linebacker in half. I smugly watched Annabeth stiffen but then surprisingly relax, hugging Beatrice back.

"Come with me, dear," Beatrice said, turning Annabeth toward her studio. "I have something special, just for you."

Annabeth looked surprised for a moment and then followed like a puppy down the hallway.

As soon as she was out of earshot, I spun toward Finn. He was busying himself, back turned watching the two women retreat.

"What is going on, Finnigan?" My voice was a vicious whisper. "Did you lose a bet with Satan or something?" Finn smiled, raising a shoulder and wiping his hands on a kitchen towel. He looked nervous. "Please tell me you aren't dating her."

"She's a good person, Swell. You could give her the chance."

"What?" My voice rose.

"She's not your enemy." His eyes were wide and hopeful. A tug moved inside me. "Please, try to be nice."

I exhaled slowly. "Are you dating her?" There was a clatter and crash as Tater barreled through the new doggy door, distracting me from the sight of Annabeth Montgomery walking into the kitchen wearing my mother's ceremonial robe.

Finnigan's face turned a sweaty, pasty white. He wasn't just dating her. My brother was in love with her.

"There should be one more joining us," Beatrice said. She was glowing, which made me feel guilty for loathing what made her so excited.

"He should be here any minute," Annabeth offered. "I bumped into him as he was leaving Spruce. He was stopping by the store to get food to bring for the solstice offering."

I froze.

"Who's getting food?" my voice squeaked. I knew before I even asked what the answer would be. Cold fear shot like lightning to my feet.

"Your man friend, dear," Beatrice said. "I invited him because I knew you were too stubborn."

My face instantly flushed. It was bad enough to share this celebration with one person who hated my guts, but two? I became hyperaware of my face, my hair, and my gangly body.

My tangled brown hair and ruddy cheeks couldn't compare to Bronson's Magical Siren of a "friend" with her long, sexy, leather-clad legs.

I looked at my reflection in the percolator. It distorted my face into a football shape. I checked my teeth and ran fingers through my hair.

"You look fine," Annabeth whispered. "You brushed your teeth, right?"

I glared at her, pinching my eyebrows into a frown. The flush in my cheeks began to burn.

"Put your hair down," she said. "And for God's sake, wear some matching underwear."

Finn joined us and asked Annabeth to pick out her solstice crown, leaving me alone to rub a finger over my teeth and scramble to my room to find a bra.

Chapter Twenty-Eight

WHAT ON EARTH would Annabeth want with Finn? He was a farmer, with no money, living with two other women in a magic commune. She hated people like us. Like Finn.

I fingered through my closet, wondering if I should pick out a matching set of underwear. I didn't want to end up standing next to the Magical Sex Barbie and know that she probably was completely sexy-matchy and I was the Black Friday Underoos special.

My reflection showed a medium-height brunette with large eyes and a calm demeanor. I wasn't too thin, but I was strong. My arms and face were tan, showing time well spent in the sun. I tilted my head to the side and watched my hair move over my shoulder like a river. I might not be an exotic, mysterious woman of the world, but I sure as hell was a woman that carried a level of confidence that trumped Little Miss Tight Pants.

I settled for clean underwear and brushed my teeth.

Annabeth wasn't like me either. Her skin was pale, a clear porcelain that looked like she'd been carved from stone. Her family had made their living using the land as a crop, to be harvested.

I thought back to Finn's smile despite myself. He'd never brought a woman home before, let alone brought someone to a ceremony. I knew this was serious, if just on his end. I smoothed my hair back, tying it into a bun, but remembered Annabeth's suggestion and loosened the knot.

The drum circle had begun in the ceremonial clearing, delivering a steady bass beat that traveled through the ground. To the people of The Row, it was a call to action. It spoke to the magic inside of me. To the braver places of me that said I could dance and speak in public.

I straightened my ceremonial dress, pressing out the remaining wrinkles from it being in storage since Beltane. The sash I wore had been my grandmother's. It fit around my waist snugly, falling at a flattering angle. I took a deep breath, looked myself in the eye one more time in the mirror, and told myself that I might not be the sexiest woman, but I was still a badass with character. "Boys like character. Right?" I asked Tater. She looked up at me, her eyebrows taking turns to challenge my conclusion.

I loved that damn dog.

I could hear people moving in the studio below me, talking and laughing. I wondered what Annabeth really thought of us, of Finn. I fought down a protective urge to warn him that she was full-on evil... But she could be genuinely interested in Finn, right?

There was no way I could know until she made her intentions known. It left me with the realization that I had to take it all with a grain of salt and keep an eye out for red flags.

As the sun began its fall into the ocean, Tater and I followed three silhouettes illuminated by the waning sun, past the garden, along the path that led into the trees. We moved in a comforting silence, mindful of where we placed our bare feet. It was a reflective meditation of our connection to the earth.

Each person had a bundle strapped to their back. We carried food, shelter, and blankets. Beatrice's sacred deerskin drum was affixed to the back of her fabric pack. The only sound she made was the clip of her walking stick thunking into the ground.

The deeper and higher we climbed, the darker our path became. At the second rest break, Finn reached into his pocket, shuffling a handful of seeds. He placed his left hand onto the trunk of an alder, clenched his right hand containing the seeds to his mouth, and blew into it, warming them up. He spoke quietly, shaking the seeds four times and then tossed them into the air. They flew upward and then stopped, hanging suspended. Finn leaned into the tree and bit down into one seed he'd kept. It snapped open, accepting the spell.

I heard Annabeth inhale with surprise as the seeds floating in the viscous air, flickered to life, glowing softly. They bobbed up and down like leaves in a pond. As Finn moved, they reacted to his location. They glided through the tree canopy above us and cast an inviting light onto the ground.

"Sweet spell, Finn!" I said, patting him on the back. I'd never seen someone transfer energy from the sun, to the trees, then to the seeds that way before.

"Hey, you're not the only one with skills," he replied and smiled sheepishly. His eyes darted to Annabeth, who reached up to touch a glowing seed. But the field around the seed reacted like water, and her attempt to touch it pushed it farther away.

"Fascinating." Bronson's voice rose from the darkened trail behind us.

"Bronson, dearest!" Beatrice's voice didn't hide her delight. "You've found us! How wonderful!"

My heartbeat jumped against my ribs.

Another shape filled the trail behind him, the last rays of sun hitting the thick curls of Samantha's hair just right. My stomach fell. She moved effortlessly like she embodied the furs that covered her.

"I thought you'd been to a solstice before," I called back. "Where's your robe?"

She didn't miss a beat. "In my bag. Never travel without it." She patted the pack with a satisfying thwomp. "Your robe is gorgeous. Heritage?"

I nodded. I didn't want to like her. Damn it.

Up ahead, Finn guided Annabeth by the hand along the trail. There was a tenderness between them that I hadn't seen in Annabeth before. In situations when she would normally be sharp and cold, she looked at him with wonder and kindness. Maybe she wasn't entirely evil. Finn was a good and loving soul, so apparently she had good taste.

Tater hung close to my feet on a natural heel. She sniffed along the edges of the pathway but didn't stray far. She looked up with large eyes and a long, happy tongue. "You're my good girl," I said. "Stay close, Tates." She wagged her tail in agreement.

I could hear Bronson directly behind me. His feet made few sounds against the soil when he stepped, but the zipper of his ranger jacket tapped against his pant leg ever so softly. It was uncanny how stealthily he moved. He'd told me he'd gone to college, but I suspected he'd also been in the military. The skills needed to know how and where to step weren't taught rifle hunting or hiking.

I closed my eyes, knowing even before I did, that I shouldn't give myself the opportunity to gain the memory.

The closer to the clearing we got, the more encompassing the drumming became. As we rose and dropped between the switchbacks and ravines that traversed a small stream and a thousand-foot elevation gain, we caught snippets of celebration following a ticker tape parade of light and people moving between the trees to the top of the mountain.

When we approached the turnoff that would take us to the spring and the lookout, Tater darted ahead and waited expectantly, assuming that we would turn at our normal spot. When we kept left instead of right, she turned quizzically to me, unsure of what I would do.

"We're going to the solstice clearing, Tater." I signaled to her, waving my hand in the direction that Beatrice, Finn, and Annabeth had taken. "You get to come with us. But remember to stay close."

"Now I get it," an amused voice said, close to my shoulder. "You talk to her like she's a human."

I turned to look at him, quickly realizing my mistake. The lights against his face, the warm smell of him—of sandalwood and fresh air—and the dangerously sexy five-o'clock shadow all pulled at me. My heart, the traitor, moved against its bars.

"She's smarter than most," I managed to say.

He grunted in agreement.

Chapter Twenty-Nine

I GULPED AND MOVED FASTER, catching up with the rest of our group. Beatrice, at the head of the pack, hummed along to the beat that pulsed through the trees. A light breeze carried the scent and smoke of the solstice bonfire to us. Memories flooded me with nostalgia as Finn's lights set the hovering smoke magically aglow.

Just behind Beatrice, I crested the hill and took in the sight of the bonfire, the dancing bodies, and small groups gathered at the edge of the clearing. An excitement bubbled up within me and I felt my inhibitions and worries dissolve. This was my turf and if Bronson and his girlfriend wanted to be here, they'd get to see what it was like to be here.

Beatrice and Finn picked a comfortable area with a few rocks for seats. It was a nook that faced east for the sunrise. Finn took the pack from Beatrice's back and began to organize the site. I helped pitch the small tent made of our discarded fabrics over the years. Nothing was wasted on The Row. The pieces of the tent were moments of our lives; Finn's work shirts, a band t-shirt, some dishcloths, the end of my mother's skirt, and my own failed attempts at sewing. I brushed the tips of my fingers across each piece, all of which were time capsules. Each spoke of my belonging. Near the edge of the tent opening, I came across a swatch of what had been one of Mark's shirts. He'd worn it to our home the first time he visited, and later I'd spilled wine on it. He'd been upset, throwing it away. But I'd nicked it from the trash and repurposed it. He'd never known because he never went to a celebration. And why would he? I'd been willing to give up this life for him... Thankfully, I'd realized my mistake in time.

I ripped the swatch off and tossed it into the bonfire.

Finn laid out a blanket for us to sit on and Annabeth distributed the celebration food from the offering foods. Once the campsite was set up and organized, Finn pointed toward the still-glowing seeds hovering above us. They gathered in a cluster, brightened, and then ignited like sparklers, cascading down small flickers of light to the waiting soil to nourish the next generation of growth.

Nothing wasted.

"Josephine Swell, you better drink up!" Beatrice nudged me as she passed her large jug of dandelion mead to the members of our small group. "The solstice waits for no one!" And with that she lit up a joint and began to smoke. "It's just herbs," she said to Bronson, waving the smoke away from him.

"I've told you before, Miss Beatrice." I could see his smile in the firelight. "I'm not a cop." He offered the jug to me.

I took it from him, trying not to stare at his hands or his face or his knee. "You may not be a cop, but you work for 'the man,' man," I said. I closed my eyes and tipped the bottle back. I took three long pulls of the mead and said, "For Beatrice, that's close enough."

I took another drink and handed the bottle to Beatrice, who offered the joint in exchange, but I waved it away. "Wine is enough debauchery for me, thanks."

"The night is young," she said and patted my shoulder before moving quickly to the basket containing the solstice crowns. She shuffled through them, handing one to everyone on the blanket. Realization dawned on me that she'd known that there would be six of us, not just three, all along.

The warmth of the wine and the festive mood lifted my spirits. I hadn't thought about Abigail, Aldo, Markus, or the glamours that I'd run headfirst into over the last few weeks. Tonight, I wanted to celebrate my hopes and dreams for a more positive year to come. I shared a piece of bread with Tater. She'd gotten comfortable and was now lazily dozing, facing the bonfire watching the dancers and drummers twirl past her. I pinched her nose gently and kissed the top of her head, leaning across to grab another nip of the wine.

Beatrice had organized the offering basket, which was filled with spring flowers and food we'd grown from our land. There were also strands of hair and sprigs of pine branches. Each item held a prayer or dream for the coming summer.

As the night passed, the solstice celebration rose to a fever pitch. The heat of the bonfire spread outward and wrapped the people in an amphitheater of warmth. I was able to remove my wool robe and feel the delightful glow of the flames against the white ceremonial dress. I wiggled my toes into the top layer of the damp soil. I knew as the night progressed, the dress would wear the blessings of another solstice.

I bent to scoop the loamy soil into my hands. I took a moment to set a personal intention of growth in the coming summer months, and then rubbed the dirt directly onto to my bare legs. It was an old tradition to bring people of The Row closer to our natural counterparts. They grew from the soil and because of that, we did as well.

Beatrice wrangled our ramshackle group into a small circle. She rolled a handful of soil, back and forth between her hands, shaping it into a pressed cone. Watching her was soothing and comforting. My head tilted to the side as I watched the flakes of minerals within the soil reflect the light of the bonfire.

It was a basic rule of existence. Energy combined with will was transferred into each granule. Once she was satisfied that the mud held the imprint of her intent, she faced each of us and sprinkled our crowned heads with newly blessed soil.

"Warmed by sun, impressed with rain.
All my prayers for the ones I love.
Take this earth, and be blessed.
May the coming days of sun
Be better than we could have ever guessed."

THE SOUNDS OF CELEBRATION CIRCLED AROUND THE bonfire, mingling within and between the concentration of magic. I laid on my back, letting my hands face palm up toward the sky. I breathed in deeply and watched the smoke of the bonfire rise like an offering to the coming sunrise.

The ground, though cool, was offset by the warmth of the fire. I would have to work hard to stay awake. I rolled onto my side and propped my head up to watch the people moving in the firelight.

When the chill of the night came, Beatrice was the first to encourage the children to begin dancing. Parents and grandparents led small hands and short legs out to dance around their first bonfire. Older children joined in, finally taking over playing and laughing with the younger children, giving the adults a break.

At midnight the ritual dances began. Everyone, including Annabeth and Bronson, participated. I couldn't help but watch Bronson interacting with everyone. He was open and cordial, even dancing with Mrs. Good, who looked like she'd lost twenty years under his attention. Mr. Good, however, wasn't as ecstatic.

There were dances of plenty and prosperity; dances to the sun and moon and the ocean, the trees that hugged the amphitheater, and the very sky we danced below. Eventually, I broke down and joined everyone dancing around the bonfire. I moved quickly past Samantha and Bronson, who interacted as only people with history together could. I danced until my mead buzz began to wear off and Elder Good began the solstice sunrise evocation. The dances that followed this prayer were the most energetically potent. Community members would pick couples deliberately, in order to hopefully pair them.

With Samantha and Bronson so chummy, I had little interest in watching them dance. I slipped between the couples, instantly awkward and aware of how single I was. I'd never been the sentimental type. I mean, I'd chosen a town over a man. What kind of person does that?

Apparently, a woman with ice in her heart and a soft spot for mutts.

At our makeshift campsite, Tater was deeply asleep in a pile of blankets and robes. The dandelion mead bottle was almost empty. I slid down onto my knees, grabbed the bottle, and crawled into the tent to drown my tween-tastic sorrows in privacy.

The fabric of the tent was illuminated from the outside and cast my little drinking den with flashes of color and shadow. I rolled onto my belly and watched from under the tent flap as they began to pair the couples.

This should be great.

I'd never gone to a school dance to spare myself this very torture. But here I was in my twenties, experiencing an awkward wallflower moment while hiding in a kid's tent.

"Old maid ... mead. Old mead," I said and I giggled. I took another long swig, tapping the bottom of the bottle for good measure.

"Josephine Swell!"

I froze. Maybe they wouldn't see me.

"Josephine Swell?" Elder Good repeated.

"She's over here!" I heard Finn say.

Once the fire stopped spinning, he was dead to me.

Beatrice's cheery face swam underneath the covers of my tent fort. "You've been selected, dear," she said. "Hurry your wallowing. There's a ceremony to do."

I grumbled and shimmied out of the tent. Sometimes there was an odd number of participants. Maybe I'd been selected to take one for the team.

But waiting for me next to Finn and Annabeth was a smug-looking Bronson Wise.

Chapter Thirty

BRONSON EXTENDED his hands toward mine. "I won't bite," he said.

"I'm not worried about you," I said.

Annabeth leaned toward me and whispered into my ear, "Maybe you should be."

"Shut up," I grumbled, but a strangled giggle escaped my chest.

The dance began clockwise around the fire. Bronson's hands were warm and firm. I wondered about the work he'd done with them. I thought of him doing trail maintenance, rescuing lost hikers... being a pain in my ass.

"You look very nice," he said, making me blush despite my best attempt to remain stoic.

The dance required the couples to link their inside arms around each other's waists and raise their outside arms up over their heads, letting their hands arch toward their partner. As our hips touched, I was suddenly aware of how thin my ceremonial dress was. I rose my arm and the belt rose too, further accentuating my chest. I cleared my throat, sobering quickly.

My left arm lightly gripped his left hip as we both faced forward, following Annabeth and Finn. My fingers, traitorous and cunning, lightly explored the waistband of his uniform. It was hard and rough, and I wondered how comfortable it could be...how it would feel against bare skin.

I shook my head, not sure if it was my own curiosity, the mead, or the dance.

The deep bass of the deerskin drums served to call the four corners to bear witness to our solstice celebration. The dance was to hold ceremonial space for two souls to acquaint themselves with one another. I'd always jokingly called it the "porcupine pairing," and now here I was, trying my best to keep Bronson at arm's length. Trying not to feel his hip and rib cage against mine, moving beneath my fingertips.

In single file now, the women guided the men. My hands rested on Bronson's narrow hips. Still in a clockwise direction, we moved one revolution around the bonfire, then turned to face each other, arms now at our sides.

"I apologize for Beatrice's meddling," I said quietly.

His eyebrows rose in surprise. "It's no problem. I've watched fertility dances before." His hand rose to my waist to follow the other couples' lead. He turned me counterclockwise to pass one revolution in reverse around the bonfire.

I could feel the heat of Bronson against the backs of my legs as the magic of the mead and ceremony thickened the air. Time moved slower.

At the apex of the circle, we faced each other once again. The sweet scent of sandalwood mingled with the bonfire smoke, and I tried to keep my shit together. The drumbeats seemed to slow, and the sound of my heart sputtered in my ears. Bronson's hands were firmly on my hips once again. The dress seemed as thin as paper in my mind now. He leaned close to my left ear. The stubble on his chin lightly scratched my jawline as he whispered, "I volunteered."

I jerked back, expecting to see a smug smile on his face, but his expression was different. He was serious. Earnest. There was a tightening in my hips.

"Oh," I said dumbly. "I didn't ... I thought ..." My eyes darted and searched for Sam.

"You thought wrong." His hand rose to my face, and his thumb rubbed my jawline where his stubble had just been. I felt the draw of his lips to mine and, for once, I closed my eyes and just let go.

TOUCHING MY BARE FEET IN THE SOIL WAS A SMOOTH stone worn flat by the creek. I bent to pick it up. I wanted to remember this moment, the exact moment Bronson had kissed me and everything felt just as it should.

He wasn't looking at me. He'd turned to watch the parade of people who cast shadows around the bonfire. Their bodies and arms moving past the fire threw bands of light onto the trunks and the bottoms of nearby branches in the trees around us.

Bronson's hair reflected the light of the fire. Strands of smooth brown thread I could still feel sliding between my fingers when I'd kissed him back. I rolled the stone in my right hand. It slid between my fingers, reminding me of the feel of Bronson's lips against mine. Color rose to my cheeks. I raised the stone to my lips, feeling energy slip into it, like a time capsule.

Someone must have seen... had to have seen us kiss.

Mine, mine, mine. I wanted him to be mine. But only time would tell.

Chapter Thirty One

As THE EARLY-MORNING hours passed by, people took turns napping while others continued to dance around the fire. Somewhere along the way my fingers became intertwined with Bronson's, and they stayed that way.

Beatrice's and Finn's eyebrows rose in my periphery, but neither said a word. My eyes searched for Samantha, who'd somehow found Elder Todd. She was talking to them animatedly, describing something that seemed to both terrify and intrigue him. I watched the way his jowls moved as he nodded in agreement. His beady eyes occasionally looked past her, flickering in the fire's reflection, while Diedre watched from the fire's edge, concerned about her new competition.

Samantha reached out and touched his forearm in an attempt to keep his attention. Maybe she had caught on to his shady vibe as well. But I had a hunch she was used to having someone's full attention.

I looked to my left, where Bronson had dozed off. He was arm deep in Tater's fur coat. She'd attempted to lie directly on him but had settled for, little spoon. I had to hand it to Tater. She knew what she liked and she wasn't afraid to let a guy know. I should have followed her example sooner.

I squeezed Bronson's hand. "Hey," I said and waited. "You awake?" He stirred, eyes fluttered open briefly. I got a firm stink eye from the pooch. "Bronson," I whispered. "It's almost sunrise."

The pull of the full moon didn't just affect the tides. It also directed the rush of the solar winds that traveled from the interior of the mountain range, carrying with them the smell of fir and green and warmth. The celebration would peak as the sun rose over the mountains, a consecration of last night's spells danced and tossed around and into the fire.

Bronson nodded but closed his eyes and leaned his face into Tater's coarse coat. She looked up at me with smug satisfaction.

I stooped to pick up an afghan in the pile of blankets, wrapping it around my shoulders. I wove through the participants of the celebration and walked to an overlook that faced southwest. From this angle, I could see the downtown area of Spruce, indicated by the slow cycle of the stoplight from Main Street and the occasional porch light. If I really focused, I could make out the silhouette of the hospital miles away. From this spot, the sound of celebration was muffled by a small patch of young trees. The solitude was comforting as I processed the weeks leading up to my make-out session with Ranger Danger.

There were many differences between us, so many ways to get hurt. But apparently my traitorous heart and libido didn't share my reasoning.

It had felt right kissing him—the ruff stubble of his jaw against my fingers, the firmness of his lips as he kissed me back. The smell of him was on my hair and against my cheeks. I wanted to kiss him again... and here I was, standing out in the middle of the woods alone. While he slept with my traitorous mutt. How had I gone from single and independent to complicated so quickly?

I pulled the knitted blanket closer to push away the night. This far from the glow of the bonfire, a cloying dampness accompanied the stiff breeze. With a start I realized I was much colder than I thought. I knew I should go back to the fire to warm up, but slowed as I stepped into a thick layer of fog rolling unnaturally from the tree line toward the clearing.

It rolled and roiled, moving like a wave, dampening the heat of the bonfire with a wet hiss. The fog and steam blocked out the moon.

I stood in shock, not fully comprehending the magic that moved around me. This wasn't a marine layer, but it wasn't common magic either. Within the cold there was a presence I could feel.

By the time I'd traced my steps back to the clearing, I couldn't see my hands in front of my own face.

"Beatrice?" I called out. "What's happening?"

"Swell!" I heard her call back, but her voice was blocked out by the deep rumble of Tater on point, who was somewhere to my west, moving and barking.

"Bronson?" I called in alarm. She'd been with him just minutes before.

"I've got her." His voice steadied the hollow thump in my chest.

I couldn't see.

I moved toward his voice. I raised one hand out in front of me while the other kept the blanket closed. The thickness of the fog pulled past my exposed ankles, fingers, and face.

Small children started to cry, startled by the harsh snarls from Tater and the sudden loss of the ceremonial fire's warmth.

I heard families gathering their belongings as they ushered their children toward the woods.

There was movement near me, something being spilled, a gasp. I reached toward a familiar scent but tripped and fell over something in my path.

"Swell!" Bronson called from across the clearing.

"I'm here!" I called back.

I searched with my hands to untangle the hem of my dress from whatever I'd fallen over. I fought a primal panic as a coppery taste blossomed in my mouth. I realized that I must have bitten my tongue when I fell.

My fingers followed the slope of the hem to the tangle—a bundle of twigs mixed with the softness of hair.

I steadied myself and leaned closer as the fog moved away for a brief moment to display the lifeless eyes of Diedre Stone.

Chapter Thirty-Two

The morning was solemn. After the Spruce Police department had arrived, interviewed, and released us from the scene, we returned to Beatrice's house in shock. We moved stiffly through the fog that lingered in the trees.

The gloom eventually pushed our ragtag group into the kitchen, where oil lamps cut a faint glow into the unnatural dim. Beatrice stood mixing a large batch of chocolate chip pancakes after throwing together a richly cheesed quiche. She slid a tray of gooey blobs into the propane stove.

We sat in shock. The only sound was the occasional scrape of a spatula on the cast iron pan or the pan sliding across the stove burner.

Tater laid below the pot-bellied stove, her eyes shifting between each of us.

I thought about taking a long hot shower, but that seemed exhausting.

I shoved myself off the stool and pulled a large metal tin down from the cupboard. I popped open the lid, and the dark, rich aroma of coffee drifted out. I liberally poured the grounds into our camping percolator, added water to the base, and snapped the strainer into place. I rifled through Beatrice's herbal cabinet and pulled out a bag of Earl Grey tea for Bronson. At least liquid happiness could be ready in a few minutes.

I darted upstairs to change out of my robe and cloak. I didn't want to put them back into the chest, worried that there could be some sort of magical juju on them. I needed to keep them out in the open until we knew exactly what we'd all walked through.

I slipped on thermal tights, with loose-fitting jeans over them. I covered a yellow t-shirt from the 2013 Turkey Trot with a thick purple sweatshirt that had the perfect hole in the right wrist to fit my thumb through. I double-socked my icicle feet, pinched my cheeks, fluffed my hair, and padded down the stairs.

I hopped over the squeaky bottom step to the wood floor landing to hear Samantha and Bronson whispering at the end of the hall. I knew I shouldn't snoop... but against my better judgment I cautiously moved toward the voices, hearing snippets of a heated conversation.

"You need to tell her..." Samantha was saying. "She needs to know about us."

"I know," Bronson hissed back. "I will tell her."

"Tell her now. It's not fair that you've kept us from her and...always...you and me..." There was rustle of fabric.

Were they hugging? They sure as shit didn't sound like JUST old friends.

I felt like I was going to be sick. I looked back over my shoulder toward the kitchen and the bright-blue kettle of boiling coffee on the stove top. It was going to be done any second. I backed up toward the kitchen, not wanting to get caught, but I was too late. There was a clatter from the kitchen, drawing the attention of Samantha and Bronson from the end of the hallway. I hated them in this house. In my home.

Samantha's expression was surprised at first, but it washed away as quickly as it had come. "Swell," she said then nodded in acknowledgment. The smell of sandalwood followed her as she passed.

"Have you been lying to me?" I asked Bronson, watching his face closely.

I wished I hadn't seen it. That flicker of unease. The change in the eyes. Bronson was hiding something from me, and even though I had feelings for him, that didn't mean he could be trusted.

"Let me explain," Bronson said as he reached his hand out for mine. "Give me a chance to explain what you heard."

Just hours before we'd been dancing around the bonfire. I'd been hopeful. But now...

"Swell!" Beatrice called from the kitchen. "Coffee's ready!"

"No more bullshit," I said to Bronson, with force. I could already feel my walls begin to rise. "Do you care about her?"

"Yes," he said. "Of course I do. She's my sister."

I wasn't expecting that. I wasn't expecting sexy legs to be related to anyone. I'd just assumed she'd grown from the tears of a succubus.

"I don't understand," I stuttered. I raised my hand to keep space between us and steady the side effects of last night's mead. "How can you be related?" I thumbed my right hand sharply to point behind me. "She's definitely

Magical."

Bronson nodded. "Our mother is Magical. But we have different fathers."

"Okay..." my voice trailed off.

"But... I'm not exactly an Ironheart, either."

"Why didn't you tell me this weeks ago?" I spat out. I felt like a fool.

He leaned forward toward me. I could tell he wanted to touch me, but I took a step back.

He sighed. "Everything I told you was true. I never lied." He looked down toward my stocking feet. Are you wearing two pairs of socks?"

"Stay on subject."

"I don't know why or how the spells work with my blood, but Samantha has a theory. I didn't come here just for the job and the land," he said.

I could feel that he was trying to carefully craft his words. "Just spit it out," I said. I could hear Beatrice taking the pot of coffee off the stove. My excuse to break off the conversation was now gone. I wanted to be anywhere but here. I didn't want to know that Bronson was an Earth Alchemist, like Markus and probably Abigail and Aldo too.

He took a deep breath and crossed the space between us to stand so close I could feel the heat radiating off of his exposed forearms. The smell of him was distracting.

"I worked for Activism United in college." His hands dug down deep into his pockets. "My sister had heard rumors about a corporation logging rare and protected timber on the coast near Spruce. She asked if I'd be open to helping, especially since I'd worked for AU before. So I've used my access to the park for the last two years to report back anything that wasn't legal."

His words were spilling out. "That's why the protesters

are here." He was smiling, relieved to be rid of the secret he'd been keeping. "The poachers I brought you in with had sawdust on their boots. It didn't take much for them to spill the beans that they were logging in the area, but they wouldn't admit where or for who."

"You've been hiding the fact that your blood, the very thing missing from Abigail's body, can affect magic?"

He looked sheepish. "I mean, do you blame me?"

I cut him off. "Enough, Bronson. An omission of fact, is a lie. You could have told me this weeks ago. You could have trusted me, maybe even prevented a child's death. But instead you withheld vital information from a Row Council officer. I don't have time for this." I headed toward the kitchen. "There's an emergency Council meeting. I can't be late."

Chapter Thirty-Three

By the time I'd walked from Beatrice's to the community hall, it was standing room only. Rows of chairs had been set up, but they'd been filled early on. Folks were packed shoulder to shoulder out into the entryway and the tiny kitchen. The room smelled of industrial-strength coffee, warm bodies, and woodsmoke.

The Row's seven Council members sat facing the room behind a makeshift table. Five men and two women were the Magical body that, in theory, represented our community's best interests to the outside world; none of whom had been out in the field in decades.

Officer Bushy Brows was in attendance. He sat near the front with Officer Trigger, who waved when he saw me. I waved in return but stayed toward the back of the building, watching. Anyone in this room could have been a suspect; not only for Diedre's murder, but for Abigail's too.

According to the preliminary report, it turned out that Diedre's death, much like her life, hadn't been magical. No spell had been used to silence her. It had been an improvised garrote of some sort that had cut off her air supply, rendering her unable to call for help. The killer had tightened the wire so hard, it had sliced into the poor woman's neck. It would have taken mere seconds for her to fall unconscious, and then a minute more to complete the job.

Poor Diedre. She'd been a snippy crab cake of a person for as long as I could remember, but that didn't mean she'd deserved to die.

Every time I blinked I could still see her eyes, speckled with the telltale purple dots of petechial hemorrhaging. They'd looked like the dappled duck eggs Beatrice had used for the quiche this morning.

I hadn't been able to eat.

"Be assured," Elder Todd said, "I will not rest until Diedre's killer is found. She was a dear friend to our community."

"What about the Steele girl?" someone called from the kitchen.

"Are our children safe?" a woman asked from the front.

"What are the Magical protocols?" the man next to her asked.

"Please, hold your questions until the end," Elder Whistanley interjected. "All of your questions might be answered if you allow us to present what we know at this time." She'd been a grade school teacher, and it showed.

"Is it true that the Steeles have left town?" Margo Eirstwhile asked as she drew her young daughter closer.

"Can they do that?" Thom Waterdown asked.

The room erupted into a riot of voices all at once.

I watched Elder Todd's face. He'd lost someone close to him, after all...

"Silence!" he boomed. His cool exterior was beginning to fray. "We'd like to invite Sergeant Jones from the Spruce Police Department to the panel. We understand the residents of our community are concerned. However, because both victims of recent events were Ironheart residents of Spruce, we must honor our agreement with our neighbors and yield to their jurisdiction regarding their own people. Sergeant Jones has generously agreed to share some information and field a few questions for us today." He stood and motioned for the sergeant to take his seat.

Eyebrows stood up and approached the panel but did not sit down. He read from a prepared release statement.

These folks were going to eat him alive.

"I heard you found her." The teenager next to me leaned over, whispering. He had a skateboard propped against his knee. "I bet you that was fucking rad."

"Kinda gross, honestly. I won't be eating scrambled eggs anytime soon."

"Huh?"

"Hey, did you know Abigail?" I replied.

"Not really. She was friends with a chick I dated a while back, though. Super quiet."

"You seen anyone unusual around here lately?"

He snorted. "You mean besides the protestors? Yeah, we're all weirdos here."

I smiled. He wasn't wrong. "Thanks, Sloane."

"Anytime."

I stepped past him toward the kitchen, where I could see Beatrice had arrived and was attempting to charm her way into a spot. She'd sidled up to a few of her yoga mates. They sipped on coffee from well-used earthenware mugs while they listened to Sergeant Bushy Brows try to convince everyone in the room that there was no immediate danger to the public. But he hadn't been at the bonfire. Everything about that magical fog and murder (Magical or not) inside our wards was a threat.

There was shouting at the door. Protestors had arrived from town. Tipped off by who? Bronson? That didn't sound right. They shouted from the back, pushing through the people at the door. This was a mess.

How were they able to pass the wards?

Officer Trigger attempted to intervene, but with the number of people in the room, he was unable to move.

"Enough!" A crack of a wooden spoon against the counter snapped across the space, and with it the static of magic.

Beatrice had spoken.

I smirked. Beatrice could have run the world if she'd had a mind to.

"Was this an act of dark magic?" Margo Eirstwhile pressed.

"That's a great question for our R&D officer, Josepine Swell," another elder offered.

The entire room focused their attention on me.

Fuck. Shit.

I cleared my throat and addressed Margo directly to help keep me from panicking. "There was definitive illegal magic accessed at the crime scene for Abigail Steele." The room stirred in concerned whispers. "The area affected by Blood Magic has since been diffused and is no longer a danger to the public. Furthermore," I continued, "as we heard from Sergeant Jones, illegal magic was not attributed to the death of Diedre Stone."

"Just spit it out! Are we safe?" someone yelled from the far corner of the room.

I looked to the Council for some sort of direction but was met with blank stares.

"There is cause for concern," I said, "as the caster has not yet been identified for Miss Steele's murder. And be aware, there are now two open murder cases under the jurisdiction of the Spruce Police Department."

The room buzzed with voices.

There were so many moving parts to think about, to anticipate... and all those parts had to navigate the bureaucracy of two different governing systems with great care.

THE MEETING ENDED ABRUPTLY WITH ELDER TODD calling it to a close.

Folks stayed in clusters, speaking in tight circles. They looked from group to group, suspicion tainting the peaceful balance that The Row was known for.

I motioned to Trigger. He regarded me with the remote-eyed tenacity of a guard dog looking for any sign of a threat.

"Did you happen to run that background I asked about?" I asked him.

"We're aware of her."

I was hoping there was something to validate the feeling I'd had since the first time I'd seen Samantha. Knowing now that she was Bronson's sister, I felt guilty. But something still didn't feel right.

"Well?"

He shifted his weight, uncomfortable and uneasy. Clearly, he didn't want to tell me what he knew. "We've had a few calls. Quite a few citizens have complained about her being dressed inappropriately."

"What?"

"It seems that pretty strangers upset the locals."

That wasn't what I'd expected. "There's nothing that came up from her background? She doesn't have a record?" It was stupid that I had to ask SPD to run backgrounds. As an R&D officer, I should have been able to access records at my discretion through The Row Council, but that was not the Council's priority.

"Just a few misdemeanors and a criminal trespass from a protest in California last year."

"Huh." It was looking like I was simply an asshole.

"Well, thanks again, Trigger. I really appreciate your expertise." The last word hurt to say. He wasn't an expert. He was a middleman for information.

"Anytime!" he said as I started to walk away. "And Swell?"

I turned around. "Yeah?"

"It's already hard enough for women to succeed in a male-dominated world. I hope you can learn to trust and encourage your female peers instead of feeling like you need to compete with them."

I wanted the floor to open up and swallow me whole. Female empowerment advice from a walking Old Spice ad?

"I'll keep that in mind," I said.

There was a commotion in the kitchen. Finn, who'd stayed back at the house had joined Beatrice where she was cleaning dishes left behind in the community kitchen. Bronson filled the space behind him in the doorway. I'd cooled off a bit and wasn't as angry with him anymore. I wondered if maybe we could go for a walk and talk?

"Is Annabeth here?" I heard Finn ask.

"No, darling," Beatrice answered. "Why would she be here?"

"I can't find her." Finn's voice cut through me. "We'd been in the garden. She stayed behind to pet the ducks while I put away the supplies. But when I went back out, she wasn't there."

A horrible feeling washed over me.

"We searched the house and outbuildings, but she wasn't there," Bronson said.

Finn shook his head. "Her truck is still in the driveway." His eyes were full of fear. Fear that I hadn't seen since we were kids.

"It's okay, Finn. I'm sure she's around here," I said, moving toward him.

"She's not, Jo!" His voice rose. "Something's. I can feel it."

I needed to distract him. "Take Beatrice home and check the garden one more time," I told him. "I'll search here."

Beatrice, taking my hint, pointed to the industrial stainless steel coffee maker and asked Finn to help her put it away.

"What can I do to help?" Bronson asked once they were out of earshot.

"Keep me company?" I asked.

He reached out for my hand. I leaned in and kissed him softly, taking in his delicious woodsy essence and the warmth of his hands.

"First thing's first. I'm going to need sugar and coffee. A lot of it."

Bronson scoured the community kitchen cupboards, finding ground coffee, a filter, and a makeshift funnel for pour-over.

"You brave enough for camp coffee?" he asked.

"Bring it," I said, shuffling through my pack for emergency sweets.

"Roger that."

I took a handful of M&Ms, chewing on their chocolately-goodness. I laid out a yoga mat from the storage closet, at the center of meeting room floor, using my bag as a pillow.

I watched Bronson move around the kitchen, setting water to boil. He then poured it counterclockwise over a tchotchke mug that said Mantra Mantra Man in bold red letters.

"Good choice," I said and pointed to the cup.

He smiled, pushing the concoction my way. "Drink up and good luck."

I tentatively brought the cup to my lips and took a sip. "Holy shit."

"Yeah?" he said, leaning his elbows on the counter. "I got tricks."

The warmth of the caffeine spread across me. I settled onto the mat and laid down while Bronson busied himself with books on a bookshelf. I closed my eyes and began to search for the essence that was uniquely Annabeth; citrus, linen, and apple blossom.

It didn't take long for my mind to lift from my body and float above the community building, The Row, and the town below. Little blips materialized—at the solstice clearing, the house, Annabeth's home, the grocery store. My mind searched the woods past Beatrice's house and lingered not far from Bronson's property—near the blue gate, where Aldo's truck had been found. A whisper of Annabeth's essence flickered in an area just beyond a ridge, where it was circled by a hundred bulbs of fire in my mind's eye—Elementals.

Chapter Thirty-Four

If there were hundreds of Elementals being summoned in Spruce, why hadn't the people of The Row noticed?

Why hadn't I felt it? How did we not know?

Bronson and I sat in his truck parked in the same spot Aldo's truck had been originally found. The fog still hung in the air, harboring a cloying chill. The forest was darker, thicker, and heavier than the last time I'd been here with Finn. I fought down my growing fear and breathed through it. These were the same woods I'd grown up in. There was nothing to be afraid of. The woods would take care of me.

Bronson and I didn't have to go far into the woods to feel the resistance of the ward. It made me want to turn away and go back to the truck. It felt like a million eyes were watching our every move, and that presence meant us every harm.

As we approached the area I'd felt Annabeth last, I could feel the massive strength of the ward. It was too strong to bring down. The key was to affect a small portion of it, not the entirety, with a distraction of energy. I moved as close to the boundary as I could, absently rolling three small stones in my pocket through my fingers. I imagined the sensation of being this close to a ward strong enough to hold hundreds of Elementals was like being on the edge of a tornado, with the pressure inside affecting the pressure outside.

The glamour of the ward reflected a still wood of spruce with an understory of thick swordfern and salal, but just past the membrane of placidity, anything could be waiting.

The stones were still cool to the touch in my pocket, but I knew that would soon change. I placed the first stone on the ground on the north side of the ward. I licked my left thumb and pressed a wet print to the top of the stone. I then took the second—a creamy off-white river stone—and set it down on the ground three feet to the south of the first so they were just a bit wider than shoulder width apart. I repeated the step of licking my right thumb and placed a print upon it.

Spit was the magic ingredient. Water, intention, and personal energy.

I licked the third stone and breathed onto it a prayer of protection and gently tossed it up into the air between the two other stones, toward the ward. I didn't hear it drop, which could be a good thing or a bad thing. The only way to know for sure would be to test it.

"Be safe," Bronson said tucking a whisp of my hair behind my ear. I savored the moment. How quickly I was growing accustomed to him with me in the woods. It was comforting to know that he would make sure Finn did not approach the ward. I needed to make sure Annabeth was there against her will before I put anyone in danger.

I waited as the stones worked against the magic of the ward—until I could see a faint shimmer of light. Translucent and ethereal, the light moved against the ward. It was the moment of truth. I took a deep breath and stepped through, feeling the magic pull against me like water draining away in a bathtub. If I wasn't careful, I could go down with it.

It took a moment to adjust to the daylight on the other side of the ward. The needles on the forest floor were so bright—defined, with such a wonderfully rich, deep orange. They were fascinating.

Time on the inside of the ward was slower, like it had been in the Elemental grove on Bronson's property. There was no fog but a heart-stopping view of raw hillside. Stumps of ancient trees sat still, jagged, and fresh. The smell of sawdust and oil hung in the air, so thick it was in my mouth and nose. Sawdust floated in the air, descending in slow motion, to the ground. The heat was intense. The membrane of the ward also served to keep everything inside —the smells, sounds, and truth of what was going on in the Mayback.

A group of men in older trucks had backed their rigs up to the freshest tract. I could see them moving slowly through the viscous environment at the bases of the trees. Methodically, they assessed each, to cut, wedge, and finally fall them. A deep popping sound of the ancient Elementals' heartwood signaled the breach. It shook the inside of me like a tuning fork. This was a slaughter of beings older than we, as humans, could ever understand.

Normally redwoods this size exploded when they made contact with the ground. But the resistance of the environment within the ward was just enough to drop the trees without damaging the wood. It increased the profits exponentially.

Two of the silhouettes that moved at the base of the trees looked familiar; my old friends Frank and Larry.

Son of a bitch.

My hands began to itch as I felt the pull of a spell crackle along the tips of my fingers. The extra juice of the ward must have lingered on my skin.

They took turns removing gear and gas cans from the back of a rusty blue-and-white truck that matched the description of Aldo's missing vehicle. Once the back was emptied, Frank closed the tailgate and the truck slowly moved toward me along the gravel road, its yellowed headlights needlessly shining in the brightness.

I slunk down behind a sword fern at the base of a freshly cut redwood, my hands sinking into its dust. I recoiled in realization as my mind registered what it was—the bone dust of an ancient being.

I frantically wiped my hands onto my wool coat, strangling a yelp.

The road brought the cab of the truck roughly ten feet from where I hid—close enough that, if the windows had been down, the driver could have heard my gasp as I saw them.

Mark listened to the radio and was singing along. Smiling as he drove through a war zone of unimaginable destruction and greed.

I stood stunned. Long after Mark had gone out of sight and I could no longer hear the gravel against the tires, I could still hear the pounding of my heart thrumming through my neck to pound inside my skull.

The access in and out of the glamour wouldn't last forever. I wasn't sure how Mark and the others were managing to pass through, but my guess was some sort of spell on the vehicles. There was a real risk of getting caught on this side without a way back through if my doorway closed. Following the path I'd taken, I worked my way back to the stone-spelled opening that sputtered like a neon sign on the fritz.

An intrusive pressure pulled against me, as I shimmied through. The heat of the ward kissed the exposed skin of my hands and face like a radiant sun. I didn't smell my own brain frying, but I knew I'd barely made it back through before the spell of the stones had been drained dry.

The stark contrast between the artificial light on the other side and the fog-drenched darkness of the forest made me night-blind. I stood still and waited for my eyes to adjust, allowing my ears and nose to make up for my lost sight. Before I was able to see the world around me, two strong hands reached out to hold me firmly by the upper arms. I hadn't heard anyone approach and was unable to keep the yelp of shock from jumping from my chest.

"Swell!" a voice whispered. "You were just supposed to take a look!"

The smell of sandalwood moved in the heavy, dark, stillness around me, and the fear I'd felt bloomed into blissful irritation. I really should put a bell on him. He was too quiet.

"Bronson? What the hell?" I spit out, startled. The shape of him began to take form. Taller than me. Wide shoulders. The rough stiffness of his jacket. I could still remember his lips on mine. I cleared my throat.

"You've been gone for almost an hour!" he said.

I thought I'd been gone no more than twenty minutes.

"Did you see her?" Finn's voice cut through the dark. Thank goodness, Bronson had been here to keep him from crossing the ward too.

"No," I said.

It was a lot to process. Mark, the slaughtering of Elementals, the poachers and their sawdust-covered clothes now made perfect sense. Coming back to this side of the ward had taken more magic than I had to offer.

"Are you okay?" Bronson asked. His voice was soft and warm, and he smelled of comfort.

I nodded, knowing that even though it was dark, he could still feel the movement. His hands dropped from my arms, and he guided me back toward the truck.

"What did you see?" asked Finn.

"There are some familiar faces on the other side." I used my hands to find my way past the foliage and unhealthy trees.

"I saw Mark," I uttered once we were safely to the gate.

"Did he see you?" Finn asked.

"No."

From behind the seat of his truck, Bronson pulled a full thermos of coffee and a Ziploc bag of brownies.

"Wow. You came prepared," I said.

He looked up and grinned, making my heart jump as I washed down a chunk of moist brownie with dark, hot coffee.

Within a few moments, my body began to warm and recover with the help of the caffeine and sugar.

"What exactly did you see?" Bronson asked.

I looked down, gathering my thoughts. "Somehow, Mark's company is summoning Elementals right under The Row's noses. Huge ancient redwoods."

"Like the ones on my property?" Bronson asked.

"Exactly." I nodded. "But it wasn't just a few. There were hundreds. And over half of them have already been logged."

"They're cutting down Elementals?" Finn couldn't hide the pain in his voice. It was a gruesome reality.

My heart was heavy as I remembered the hollow drumbeat of the heartwood breaking in the redwood as it fell. "They aren't able to protect themselves."

"What can we do?" Bronson asked. My heart squeezed as he used the word *we*.

"I'm not sure," I said. "But I think it's time Aldo answered some tough questions."

Chapter Thirty Five

I DIDN'T THINK Mark was pulling this off on his own. He'd once used dish soap in the front-load washer. When the bubbles filled up the laundry room, he'd turned off the machine and failed to mention it until I got home. In college, he'd let a carton of milk spoil. Instead of throwing it away, like a normal person, he'd left it in his dorm room fridge when he moved out. Thinking back on it... that really was some evil mastermind shit.

Crystals of moisture spun through the headlight beams as Bronson guided his truck through the dim, toward the Hungry Hollow Trailer Park. I looked out into the dark to the trees beyond, knowing now that not even a mile away, magic was being used for profit.

Annabeth was in danger.

I was sick to my stomach.

Bronson's hand reached out to cover mine. His voice cut through the dark and warmed away the fear inside me. "We'll find her."

I thought about seeing Mark behind the wheel of Aldo's truck. It all felt like a bad dream—that someone I'd trusted could have changed or hidden so much all those years. Reflexively, I rubbed my free hand against my pant leg. I could still feel the Elemental's dust under my nails.

The spell that hid Aldo and the ward that encircled the Redwoods were similar. They served to hide what was inside a specific boundary. The very magic used, imbalanced the area around it. The time difference inside the ward and the emaciation of Aldo's own body was a magical fingerprint.

All the lights were on at Ilene's. The kite fans spun slowly in front of her porch, that was drenched by floodlights.

She opened the door before I knocked.

"Saw you coming..." she said, stepping out through the screen door. "Hard not to see everything with these damn lights on."

Ilene was wearing a pastel-mint house robe and pink velvet slippers that flipped as she shuffled to the kitchen. She leaft the door open behind her.

"Why don't you just turn them off?" I asked, stepping inside. Finn and Bronson followed close behind.

"I'd love to, but they're motion activated," she said. One unlit cigarette was pinched between two of the fingers on her right hand. "And the damn crows keep setting them off. I was tired of my yard flickering like a damn disco, so I just turned them on to stay."

She pulled an empty glass ashtray toward her on the kitchen counter. "Little bastards." A jar of Folger's crystals and a can of powdered creamer sat on the counter. My stomach clenched in protest. Nothing within arm's length of Ilene was healthy.

"I didn't see any crows," Bronson said.

"Well, you must have scared them away with your muscles, sugar." Ilene smiled at Bronson and leaned against the counter, revealing all of her teeth. She reminded me of a cat courting its meal. "They've been congregating outside like ants at a picnic."

She took a sip from a thin white cup that reminded me of candy marzipan.

"How are the patients?" I asked, looking past her toward the living room.

"Not eating enough," she complained.

I could hear Markus move on the couch as the "protective" plastic cover crinkled beneath him. That must have been making him hella sweaty. It wasn't exactly a breathable fabric, and he wasn't exactly mobile.

"I've gained five pounds!" he called out.

Aldo was sitting in the velvet rocking chair Ilene had sat in the first time I visited. The size of the chair dwarfed him. But he looked energetic despite the shadows under his eyes. "Any news?" he asked before we'd even made it into the living room.

"Well," I began. "Funny you should ask..." my voice trailed off, as I wasn't sure how to broach the subject. "We've just come from the Mayback."

Aldo's gray eyebrows rose like caterpillars.

"Did you ever come across any redwoods, Aldo?" I asked, deciding to be direct and honest.

After some hesitation, he nodded. "The first time I saw them, there were only a few. A small grove just north of the Mayback. I slept there for a couple nights. It was warmer and I felt safe. But they were gone within a couple days. I don't know... I thought maybe that was normal on The Row?" He scratched his head, disrupting a patch of wild hair. "But," he said with a sigh, "I was also kind of worried that I'd done it somehow. You see, I'd fallen and torn my pants."

"What would you tearing your pants have to do with all this, Aldo?" I asked.

A deep furrow formed between his eyebrows. "You see, I was bleeding..."

Bronson moved behind me to sit at the end of the couch next to Markus, whose purple toes peeked out from the end of his leg cast.

Aldo's face held so much guilt that I wanted to give him a hug. "Aldo, if your blood effected a spell or ward, I need to know," I told him.

He nodded. "I remember spruce needles and dirt getting stuck to my finger because I'd used my hand to brush off my leg. I can still see the burnt red needles stuck to the blood on my palm. One minute I was scrambling away from those crows, and the next I was under three large trees. The largest trees I ever did see." His hands squeezed his knees, as if to work out a pain deep inside his bones. "There was a popping sound, and the needles on the ground rose up," he paused. "I should have been scared, but they were so darned beautiful, those trees. Like they had come to shelter me. And I was so tired."

I remembered Bronson's blood on my blade. The single drop sliding down to sink quickly into the soil. That ward had probably been the product of Aldo's fear. But Bronson's blood made it far more potent.

"Aldo, have you always known you were different than other Sprucers?" I asked.

He scratched his beard and rocked back and forth in the

chair. "Yes, ma'am, I sure did. Never met anyone else like me and Markus, till now."

"What about you, Markus? I asked. "Anyone else know you were different?"

He shook his head, no. "The only thing that made me special was I always grew the best weed."

"We don't need to know that," I said, pointing to Bronson.

"He's a just a ranger, Swell," Markus replied. "He's cool."

I heard Bronson snicker.

I needed to find a quiet place to focus and see if Annabeth's location had changed.

"Ilene," I asked, "do you mind if I use the ladies' room?"

She cocked her head to side and sized me up. "We flush in this house."

I chanced a sideways glance at Bronson and Finn. Neither tried to hide their amusement.

"Yes, ma'am," I said.

"Last door on the right," she called after me. "And light a match!"

That woman was a master of psychological warfare.

We huddled around the coffee pot and hatched a plan.

"She's still there," I said.

"Are you sure?" Finn asked. He'd been pacing back and forth across Ilene Frank's kitchen so much that he'd made her nervous.

"Either he has to sit down, or ya'll are going to have to

leave," Ilene said. "He's wearing a path across my freshly Mop and Glo-ed floor. And that stuff ain't cheap."

"Sorry, ma'am," he said.

"Miss," she reminded him.

I cleared my throat. "We don't have much time to do this. Mark needs the ingredients now, otherwise he wouldn't have taken her."

"Anyone on the Council could be involved." Bronson spoke aloud my fear.

He was right. Anyone who was at the solstice celebration, anyone Magical—even anyone with enough influence to help hide such a large operation—could be helping him.

I thought about Annabeth and how she'd looked with such wonder at Finn's spell the other night.

Being sentimental wouldn't get her to safety. Only the element of surprise would.

Chapter Thirty-Six

HIKING stick in hand and weighed down with a small arsenal of stones, we walked into the sickly spruce grove. A scurry of movement deeper in the woods gave away the location of three crows moving around the area I'd broken through the ward, not long before.

Bronson, Finn, and I would need to backtrack and cross closer to the road to avoid them. I worried if Mark or anyone else passed by on the roadway they might be able to see the disturbance in the ward's membrane. We couldn't afford to be stuck on the inside without a way out, especially if Annabeth was injured.

The roadway.

"Mark must have used the vehicle to move through the ward," Finn said.

"Or the road's a glamour," I said.

"Let's not chance it," Bronson replied.

I looked at the space above the roadway, sizing it up. I broke off a piece of Bronson's last brownie and tossed it directly four feet above the center of the lane, and immediately regretted my decision. It crackled on impact like a fly in a zapper.

That was a perfectly good brownie.

"Well, that won't work," Finn said.

"Definitely not," Bronson agreed.

I set the first stone on the ground as far from the road as I safely could; the second stone positioned three feet away. Each placed with intention and sealed with a lick to the thumb with a print. To the third stone I spoke my intention before bringing it to my lips. I tossed it higher than last time, to accommodate Bronson and Finn.

The ward shimmered and fell away between the stones. The opening was much larger than the last and might be easily seen from the road. But it was too late to change that.

We took turns passing through. Finn first, then Bronson, and finally me.

The magic pushed against me and pulled at my guts. It took a few moments to acclimate to the brightness on the other side of the ward.

The clearing hung thick with magic. The redwoods rose high above the dwarfed silhouettes of people, who worked quickly at their bases. They moved between the trunks like ants. Some alone and some in pairs.

Finn pointed toward Aldo's truck parked in the distance. I couldn't hear an engine running over the ringing tones of mauls connecting to the blunt ends of the wedges.

Mark was nowhere to be seen.

What would I say to him, when I found his evil ass? How would it feel to see him face to face? Mark had been good once, hadn't he?

But that hadn't helped Abigail, or Annabeth for that matter. Their blood was a commodity that the new-to-me

Mark couldn't waste. He needed it in order to finish this slaughter before The Row came down on his operation.

A dark form darted from where we'd crossed. It was a familiar shape that stooped with the history of logging. Aldo, moved with the agility of a seasoned choke setter, directly into the grove, followed by a pulsing shadow of crows that fought against the gelatinous consistency of the magic encircling the trees.

"Shit," I hissed. I raised the hiking stick, biting the end of it to symbolize an action, and slammed the end into the soil, moving the spell through the ground and air. The sensation of the wood against my teeth echoed inside me as my intention to separate the crows from their subject slid through the atmosphere. The taste of alder and sand bloomed on my tongue, and the crows, confused by the lack of focus on a target, hovered for a moment and then intersected. Small black bodies converged and darted through the ward, to the world outside.

What was Aldo doing?

Bronson signaled his change in direction, traveling silently across the distance, hidden by a tangle of slash.

But we weren't the only ones to have noticed Aldo.

A lithe form moved out of the shadows. Samantha, robed in all her animal skin bad-assery, followed Mark toward the sea of jagged stumps, her eyes set on the old timer, crossing the tangles in front of her.

Mark smiled wide at her in adoration.

Her fingers stretched outward as she raised her hand toward Aldo. Without touching him, she lifted him into the air and with a flick of her wrist, Aldo's body flew like a rag doll through the air.

His form slumped at the base of a smoldering slash pile. Fear and pain rose through me, escaping in a scream that oozed around me, distorted by the ward. He should never have been here. He should have been safe. Guilt broke open inside me. He'd followed us through the open path.

Aldo's small frame didn't move. It laid still and thin like a clump of discarded clothing. A voice inside me spoke of revenge, to balance the scales. To tip the favor. To save what remained of the redwoods and avenge Aldo.

I was going to make Samantha pay.

Chapter Thirty-Seven

MOVEMENT across the trunk-scabbed surface drew my eye away from Aldo's body to my old buddy, Poacher Frank. He pushed Annabeth Montgomery, still dressed in ceremonial white, out into the clearing. Her face was calm, but a bruise—already purpling—stood out against the paleness of her skin. The collarbone of my mother's ceremonial dress was stained with a mix of fresh red and a dried brown.

Frank's little buddy, Larry, wasn't too far behind. He jabbed Elder Todd to move forward with the business end of a familiar rifle. The elder's shirt was rumpled and stained. Dark circles framed his eyes, that hid behind swollen eyelids. He glanced upward to the bright sky.

The ward glimmered and rippled as three crows slipped through the magic like knives. They swept wide. Two landed on a fresh stump. The third landed on Samantha's outstretched arm; revealing the blood magic caster's identity with a dramatic flair.

I knew I didn't like her.

Elder Todd's shoulders slumped. He shook his head

back and forth as Little Larry nudged him forward, with a sharper jab this time.

I couldn't hear what they were saying.

My whole body vibrated with the raw energy in the clearing. I navigated between the ferns and bushes, to get closer, catching tidbits of their conversation. I darted around large piles of broken branches and other wood debri, to the southernmost point of the expanse. I crouched down closer to Mark, who leaned casually against the front of the truck. Oblivious to me being so close.

Just like old times.

From this vantage I could see Frank's tight grip on Annabeth's forearm. The goose egg on her cheek looked painful.

"No going back for you now," Mark said to Elder Todd. "This is just the beginning." He handed Elder Todd a knife sheathed in leather. "A life for a lifestyle. You'll be a rich man!"

"You're all pathetic," Annabeth said. Her words pulling Mark's attention.

"You see?" Mark spat, sweat damped his button up shirt. "This is exactly what I'm talking about! Smug fucking Sprucers casting judgment on anyone who isn't JUST LIKE THEM!" His lips moved awkwardly around his teeth, enunciating each of the last three words. "Well, I'm not just like them! I'm better than them. Smarter. Faster. Richer!"

"That's right, love," Samantha purred. Her hair moved around her face, like it was alive. "You're better than this shit town."

Annabeth pulled at Frank's grip. "Swell was right about you; about both of you," she said to Mark.

Mark's face twisted as he crossed the short distance to

where Annabeth received the back side of his hand.

Blood bloomed on her lower lip. But instead of crying, she began to laugh—a full, gut-pulling laugh. "Mark, you can't even do magic without them! How could you be BETTER than them?" She was laughing harsher now.

"You mean like with the help of your boyfriend?" Mark snapped back.

"Finn would never help you," Annabeth said, shaking her head. She spit blood onto the ground.

"Who do you think gave me the idea?" Mark said.

"You're a liar."

"Careful, Annabeth. You're starting to sound just as unhinged as he was that day in the cafeteria."

Cafeteria? The memory of Finn's fingernails pressing red half-moons into his palms flashed in my mind.

Finn had used Blood Magic that day. We'd never talked about it. We'd been kids grieving, but my memory expanded to the boy Finn's magic had held up off the ground; Mark.

Finn had almost killed him, without even laying a finger on him.

"Kill her! Mark screamed. But Elder Todd shook his head and dropped the knife. He pulled away but was stopped short by the butt of little Larry's shotgun connecting to the back of his head.

"I have to do everything!" Mark screamed and reached down for the blade that laid near Elder Todd's still body.

Time sped up as the glamour flickered. The magic was puttering out. He needed to refresh the power source it fed from. I stood and slid the heavy pack off and squared my feet. Before I could reveal myself, the knife flashed silver in Mark's grip as it connected with Annabeth's stomach, driving the blade deep. I screamed and witnessed in sick slow motion as Annabeth fell.

Chapter Thirty-Eight

DEATH CUT through the clearing and carved a line between what came before and all that would never be. The red halo of Annabeth's life spread outward. The magic in her veins sung to the spell that was not yet complete. I could still feel her through the trees. They were with her. She wasn't gone, but she wasn't here either.

Chaos erupted. Bronson and Finn moved in slow motion, navigating the scarred terrain. We were all too late. I stood helpless.

I felt Mark's gaze the moment he spotted me out in the open. Beyond the macabre scene, redwoods that had already been wedged, cut, and broken continued their slow descent to the forest floor. They popped and groaned through the thickness of the flickering ward.

It was just enough distraction for Mark to make his move—to strike. His body, not affected by the ward's magic, moved blindingly fast, getting to me quicker than I could react. He barreled into me, my hiking stick clattering away.

The force of him lifted me off of my feet, knocking the air from my lungs. It brought colors behind my eyelids; red of the ripest raspberries, green of the tender huckleberry leaves, white of the brightest day after the darkest winter. The ground waited. The duff that surrounded the Elementals' redwood grove was soft and pliant. It wrapped itself around me, while I took deep, desperate, sucking breaths that failed to fill my lungs.

"You're killing people and cutting down trees?" Bronson's voice rose to reach his sister through the heaviness. "Why, Sam?"

"Have you seen the price of real estate, lately?" she asked. "If I want to make change, real change, I'll need money."

I raised myself onto my hands and knees. A wave of anger forced its way through the chill of shock. My lungs got purchase and I was able to breath again.

"Sacrifice a few, to save the many..." Samantha said.

My vision traveled outward slowly from a small pinpoint. The trees above us jerked side to side, their limbs bending in a downward twirl. I had to move.

I felt Mark circle me, his spittle spraying as he ranted. I squinted to look for him. His skin was thin. Dark circles pulled below his eyes. Ironhearts weren't supposed to be exposed to magic like this. It wasn't good for them. By the looks of it, the toll wasn't just on the body but on the mind.

The familiar rasp of my hiking stick against the ground drew my attention.

"What did you always say? Intention is everything," He spat. He tossed my stick from his left hand to his right. "To most people, this would just be a stick. But with intention?" Mark laughed as the shaft whistled through the air and made direct contact with my left shoulder.

"Intention is everything."

Pain exploded in my body. I refused to cry out. Mark wouldn't get anything more from me.

"Not so strong now!" I heard Mark sneer. "Not so tough now! Are you?" He seemed to rise off the ground in jubilation.

"Swell!" Bronson shouted. He was too far away.

My left arm was useless, filled with what felt like fire ants reaching to my fingertips. I rolled onto my right side, sliding my hand around a stone in my pant's pocket, as the stick made contact again with my wounded arm.

Frank and Larry tackled Bronson in the distance as my mind took me from the grove to a winter solstice almost four years past.

On that night, the dark sky of sprinkled stars had winked as Mark had asked me to move with him to the city and I'd accepted. We'd been so happy and hopeful. And in that moment, I'd picked up a smooth stone from the ground and laid the memory into it. To share with our children one day.

But instead, that memory, buoyed the hope inside me now as I brushed the fingers of my right hand past the stone in my pocket. It dulled the pain just enough and I staggered to my feet. The world was a roar of sound and color.

I pointed my finger to the ground, moving my will through the soil to Mark, whose eyes reflected the gray clouds above us. I thought of what we'd been through, what we'd shared, and I felt sadness for a brief moment before I spoke one word to him.

"No."

It struck him by surprise. His expression of betrayal burned into me. He blinked, and the euphoria was gone—replaced with anger. He raised the stick again.

My fingers curled against the touchstone. The cool serenity of it broke inside me.

"No." The stone snapped in two.

He stumbled backward. The hiking stick falling to the ground and I bent to pick it up.

"I'm sorry, Mark, but you did this to yourself."

He unleashed a growl that made the hair on the back of my neck rise.

So many players moved around us. So many pieces in play.

First Mark, then Samantha.

The ward faltered. Daylight sputtered to night and back again.

An Ironheart had worked magic, had taken a life. Balance had to be restored...

I felt the bullet before I heard the report of the gun. It seemed that Poacher Frank still held a grudge for me taking his dog and had taken his shot at getting even. It reminded me of the time I'd sliced my finger in the kitchen as a child. The delay in pain arrived on a wave of nausea. It surprised me as the underside of my hand push down onto a hole that spread red across my stomach.

I couldn't maintain the spell that bound Mark if my own will was ebbing away. My hands were clubs of meat, unable to hold on to my stick. It landed softly as I staggered, my legs no longer obeying my mind.

More than anything, though, I felt regret. Regret for leaving Beatrice and Finn behind. For never really treating Bronson with the respect he deserved. I hadn't been able to save Aldo or Annabeth, Diedre or Abigail. It was all so very sad.

So much death, for what? Money? Power?

Mark's pupils dilated. He was mad, not angry or hurt,

but truly undone and raw with the very thing he hated. Magic.

I couldn't fight the pull of fatigue anymore. My knees were soft, and I swayed, tipping toward Annabeth.

Who brings a gun to a magic show? Fucking poachers, of course.

Death was so messy. The cloying dampness that covered my own stomach, mirrored the cloud of Annabeth's blood that spread thickly across and through the grains of soil. Between the dainty redwood needles and pulpy sawdust clumps, it sizzled toward me like a slow-moving tsunami, and I watched, my eyes wide open in wonder.

Annabeth's face was pale gray. Maybe my face looked just like hers, now. Then, a flicker of movement.

Did her fingers move?

My lungs were spongy. It felt like I'd been skewered straight through with a hot poker. I rocked my body to sit up, but fire bloomed in my belly. I realized that the bullet must still be inside me. I reached outward, bracing myself to breathe through the wet tissue inside my chest, and felt my hand slide into Annabeth's lukewarm blood. Before I could find purchase in the coagulated halo, my mind flashed bright white.

I WAS THE EARLY-SUMMER WILDFLOWERS THAT FILLED THE old lumber yards. I was the delicate pollinators. I was the seed. I could feel the heavy summer sun and the stillness of the longest winter day. I was now and then. I was everything. The taste of the sunlight. I was the soil, the broken-down parts of the magical minerals of the soil.

Absently, I thought I must have died. That my process of

learning the secrets of the universe had begun. I had unraveled.

No. I was being woven tighter into the fabric of home. The shallow spruce roots. The hard conks. I could see the process of growth in small segments. The slow building and structuring within the newest rings in the oldest trees. I was the new growth sprouting outward, gangly like a newborn fawn. I was the eagle, its talons sharpened through years of purchase and prey.

Life bent like a rainbow.

I FELT MY FINGERS, WET AND STICKY, SPRINKLED WITH evergreen needles, as my consciousness returned to my body. My awareness pushed outward to the edges of the ward, against the boundary that was losing its power.

Neither Mark nor Samantha had finished the spell, which meant there was still time.

All at once my awareness snapped back, pulling with it, the thick, alchemical essence that made Annabeth's blood and the blood of others like her so unique. It held the key to change the rules of magic.

It held the power to save a life.

With the last of my will I focused on the point in my belly—the tiny intent that existed to end my life—and pulled it outward. It felt just as horrible coming out as it did going in. In tiny increments the bullet moved backward, coming to rest in the palm of my hand.

I squeezed my eyes shut and imprinted this moment into the bullet. A smoky gray of potential, it compressed the laws of physics with the chemistry of magic.

THE ENERGY CURLED, PINCHING TIGHT LIKE A ROSE, ITS power terrifyingly beautiful. The shimmering petals of magic pulsed as the spell continued to compress into itself, compacting the energy into an explosive nothingness that ate everything around it. Until at last, in a blindingly euphoric moment, the bud imploded, pressing those of us within range outward with its impact.

The blast lifted me, weightless. I watched in detached awe as the trees moved in segmented order to the concussion. They swayed. They danced. They trembled.

I landed harshly against the sharp debris. Needles rained down. They fluttered delicately in lazy pathways to the ground, now free of the ward. My chest was on fire. It screamed for air that came in shallow breaths, stained with the taste of citrus and freshly pulped redwood.

The commotion of bodies pressing and shoving through the atmosphere grated like sandpaper against my skin.

I could feel Finn lifting Annabeth, the unmoving vacancy in Aldo, and Samantha moving away from Bronson. His calls to her were swallowed in the ringing of my ears.

I rose thickly and clumsily to my knees, my left arm numb and useless; my hips stiff. I placed my good palm to the soil and, with a whispered apology, pulled energy up from the closest remaining redwoods. I'd expected only a little help, but the power that rose up through me was hot as fire and sweet as coastal air. It moved like electricity and propelled me upward, to my feet.

Mark's eyes grew wide. He'd thought I was dead. Did he feel sadness or remorse? I didn't know. We stared at each other as the ward fell with an audible crack, releasing time to its natural speed. The heavy-trunked redwoods, with their thick, springy bark and delicate needles, reacted to the new law of gravity. It pulled them faster than Mark could have foreseen. I watched helplessly as the very Elemental, Mark's actions had slated for harvest, laid its final judgment squarely upon his body.

The landing site was a blast zone of debris. There was no way Mark could have survived. His punishment had been swift at the Elemental's discretion.

Chapter Thirty-Nine

After the ward fell and the spell slowly faded, the remaining Elementals lingered for a few days; long enough for people to mingle at their great bases and wonder at their crowns. And just as quickly as they'd come, they were gone, leaving behind a field of wildflowers that smelled of lemon zest and cherry blossoms.

After the Council released us from the crime scene, Bronson brought me home. Beatrice and Tater were a beacon of warm light in the dark night. I folded myself into bed and slept for two days. The wounds were gone, but the energy I'd used left a tenderness behind.

Samantha was in the wind. Each shadow that passed my window made me flinch. She and her winged familiars could be anywhere by now.

Trigger came by to get my statement. He said that Elder Todd had admitted that Samantha and Mark had approached him months before, offering to pay him for his silence. In turn, The Row would be able to buy the land to the south after it was logged.

Bronson visited every day. We watched movies and

walked Tater in the woods. Summer had arrived, and with it the sweet smells of warm soil and fresh sap.

Samantha was Bronson's sister and, though he loved her, he'd seen the darkness she was capable of.

The woods were a good place to grieve and heal. To try to make sense of so much death.

Abigail. Diedre. Aldo. Mark.

We would never know Mark's motivation or the depths of his participation.

And Aldo. My guilt held his memory like a fire.

Late on the fifth day, we got word that Annabeth was being released from the hospital. We met for coffee at The Goose. Finnigan left Annabeth and I to talk while he got coffee, but we didn't speak. We just held hands and looked out the window to where Tater stood guard, watching the mundane moments of Spruce pass by.

Across the street, sunlight warmed the tops of trees in the city park. Below the canopy, birds of all sorts flittered between the branches; blue jays, scrub jays, wrens, robins, and three uncanny crows that perched within the shadows and just out of sight.

Summer

My Dearest Children,

The Row is a magical place, where trees touch the sky, the mountains tip lazily into the ocean, and thick, cool fog lays on the ground to sleep each night.

It is also a place that must be protected from those who are unable to see past their screen of greed and ego. It must be safeguarded from those who do not see the woods as living and cannot fathom their true worth beyond money.

Many will come to harvest our magic like berries from the vine, but we mustn't let them. We must resist.

Our home is a source of safety and courage. Life and love may pull us from The Row, but The Row can heal us, rejuvenate our spirit, and heal a broken heart.

Never be afraid to come home—but also don't be afraid to leave. For magic is in our blood. And because of that, we can never be truly gone, or lost, or missing. We are home, infinitely.

Love,

Your Mother

Author's Note

The climate crisis is more apparent than ever with unprecedented wildfires, flooding, and natural disasters linked to global warming throughout the world. Though, The Row and Spruce are fictitious places, the dangers of greed and self interest are very real.

As a child, I watched Saturday morning cartoons next to sawdust-covered boots. I eavesdropped on heated conversations regarding the spotted owl, environmentalists, and loggers during the Timber Wars.

As an adult, I grew to see the devastation poor forest practices have on community economics and natural ecosystems in the long run. These pivotal moments in Oregon history made a huge impression on me and greatly influence my writing.

I wrote *Summoning Spruce* for those kindred spirits who seek the magic that only nature can offer; the activist at heart, the tree-sitters, the environmentally conscious, those who endeavor to benefit their community through leadership or empathy, and for those who are a little witchy on the DL.

About the Author

ANN ORNIE is an Oregonian, lover of old trees, the desert, and is a National Park enthusiast. When she isn't writing or reading she can be found rambling through the woods on an adventure with her husband, son, and dog named Lucy.

She is the writer and producer of the Cold Coast Podcast, dedicated to the missing and unidentified persons of the Pacific Northwest. You can visit her website at: www.annornie.com or follow her on Instagram: @treesifyouplease.

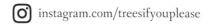

instagram.com/treesifyouplease

Made in the USA
Middletown, DE
22 June 2023

33233279R00139